Also by Cal Ripken, Jr.
with Kevin Cowherd

Hothead
Super Slugger

a novel by

CAL RIPKEN, JR.

with Kevin Cowherd

Disney • Hyperion Books

New York

As always, a special thanks to Stephanie Owens Lurie,
Editorial Director of Disney-Hyperion Books, a wonderful editor
and friend. For all our books, she's the straw that stirs the drink.
—K. C.

First Edition
10 9 8 7 6 5 4 3 2 1
G475-5664-5-13025
Printed in the United States of America

Library of Congress Cataloging-in-Publication Data
Ripken, Cal, 1960–
Wild pitch/a novel by Cal Ripken Jr.; with Kevin Cowherd.
p. cm.
Summary: "Robbie Hammond, the Dulaney Orioles pitcher, has to
persevere through a losing season"—Provided by publisher.
ISBN 978-1-4231-4002-3 (hardback)
[1. Baseball—Fiction. 2. Self-confidence—Fiction. 3. Perseverance
(Ethics)—Fiction. 4. Secrets—Fiction.] I. Cowherd, Kevin. II. Title.
PZ7.R4842Wil 2013
[Fic]—dc23   2012020721

Reinforced binding

Visit www.disneyhyperionbooks.com

SUSTAINABLE FORESTRY INITIATIVE   Certified Sourcing
www.sfiprogram.org
SFI-00993

THIS LABEL APPLIES TO TEXT STOCK

For the beautiful Madeline Chloe Cowherd.
One day, she'll know why.
—Kevin Cowherd

Robbie Hammond stared in at the batter and tried to look intimidating. I need to work on my game face, he thought. Hitters don't dig in against a pitcher with a good game face. Mine is lame. When I try to scowl, I look like a kid who needs to find a bathroom in a hurry.

He vowed to practice in front of the mirror when he got home, if his little sister wasn't around to watch. It was hard to concentrate with Ashley cackling and shouting, "Mom, you gotta see this!"

Robbie got the sign from his catcher, Joey Zinno, and nodded. He went into his windup, kicked, and fired. The pitch was low and outside, but the Tigers batter swung anyway and missed for strike one.

"Yes!" Joey shouted, pointing at Robbie before whipping the ball back. "Now you're dealing!"

Robbie exhaled slowly. Maybe that last pitch wasn't a thing of beauty, he thought. It didn't exactly split the plate. But it was the best one he'd thrown all day, which wasn't saying much, seeing as how the Orioles were getting their butts kicked—again.

He glanced at the scoreboard behind the center field fence: Tigers 5, Orioles 0. And it was only the fourth inning, meaning there was still plenty of time for further disaster. Gazing at the stands, Robbie saw that the Orioles' cheering section wasn't exactly riveted by the action on the field, either. Two dads were talking on their cell phones. Another was pecking away at his laptop. One mom had her head buried in a book.

Even a couple of dogs tied to the fence looked bored. That's how bad we are, Robbie thought. We even make pets yawn.

Still, as he wiped the perspiration from his brow, Robbie permitted himself a thin smile. At least he hadn't given in to the batter. He'd gone after him, challenged him with his best pitch. He hadn't walked him, the way he had with four other batters so far.

Then he heard it.

"BEND YOUR KNEES! FOLLOW THROUGH!"

There it was again. The same voice he'd been hearing since the season started two weeks ago—an annoying fog-horn that conveyed more than a hint of impatience. If the voice had belonged to a kid, Robbie would've wanted to gag him and shove him into a closet.

The problem was, the voice belonged to his dad.

Robbie glanced over at the Orioles dugout. Ray Hammond was perched on the top step in his usual pose: shoulders hunched, hands jammed into the pockets of his blue Windbreaker, rocking back and forth on his heels. A thick man with a buzz cut under his O's cap, he chomped furiously on a wad of gum the size of a golf ball.

Watching him, Robbie was glad his dad hadn't discovered the joys of chewing sunflower seeds. The man would be spraying them like machine-gun fire about now.

"CONCENTRATE! PUT THIS GUY AWAY!"

Robbie sighed. Give it a rest, Dad, he thought. Let me at least enjoy this rare moment of triumph before I uncork one that sails over the backstop this time.

But his dad wasn't about to stop yapping, Robbie knew.

No, as the new coach of the Orioles, his dad was a nervous wreck. Outwardly, Ray Hammond could fool you. As a Baltimore cop, he projected an air of calmness and authority. And why not? In his sixteen-year career, he'd been decorated numerous times for coolness and bravery in the line of duty.

Just a few months ago, he had answered a call about a domestic dispute and stood in a kitchen, across from a distraught man waving a knife. It took over an hour, but eventually Robbie's dad talked the guy into putting down the knife and surrendering. For that, Sgt. Hammond was awarded the Bronze Star, one of the police department's highest honors.

No, there wasn't much that seemed to rattle Ray Hammond—until he took over the Orioles. Here he was less certain of himself, Robbie knew, still finding his way as a rookie coach. And it didn't help that his kid, supposedly the best pitcher on the team, couldn't find the strike zone with a GPS. Or that the Orioles weren't hitting, either, and kept discovering new and innovative ways to lose.

Maybe the rest of the Orioles couldn't tell, but Robbie

knew his dad was stressing in his new role. And one way Coach Hammond dealt with the stress was to bark nonstop advice to his players, in a voice you could hear in Canada.

Coach Motormouth, some of the kids called him when they thought Robbie couldn't hear them. But Robbie heard everything—everything his dad said, and everything his teammates said, too. Which was part of the problem.

"JUST RELAX OUT THERE!"

Oh, that's helpful, Robbie thought. Telling a pitcher who's wild and down 5–0 to relax. A little late for that, isn't it?

Besides, if you *yelled* at someone to relax, didn't it have the opposite effect?

Wouldn't it be better to use a soothing voice—your indoor voice—to calm your rattled pitcher?

No wonder baseball wasn't nearly as much fun this season. Even though he was short for his age, with stubby arms and legs that he feared made him look like SpongeBob, Robbie had always been the best pitcher at every level he played. "You got a live arm, son," his coaches had always said.

At the prestigious Brooks Robinson Camp last summer, he had mowed down one batter after another in the intrasquad games. Brooks Robinson himself, the great Hall of Fame third baseman, had watched from the sidelines and said to one of the coaches, "The boy sure has some giddyup on that fastball."

But that was then.

That was before *it* happened. The thing with Stevie Altman.

Oh, Robbie still had plenty of—what was it again?—"giddyup" on his pitches. He still threw harder than anyone else in the league. But lately, more often than not, he had no idea where the ball was going when it left his hand.

And now that the Orioles had lost their first six games of the season, his dad was barking at him a lot. Which didn't seem to happen to any of the other Orioles, Robbie noticed.

Now the Tigers batter dug in again. But this time he was crowding the plate, hunched over the inside corner as he waved his bat menacingly in the air.

Seeing this, Robbie froze. Shouldn't the kid step back a little? Wouldn't that be the smart thing to do? Shouldn't he tuck that elbow in so he doesn't—?

"Time!" a voice behind him yelled. Willie Pitts, the Orioles' speedy second baseman, trotted to the mound. He was joined by Connor Sullivan, the big shortstop, and Jordy Marsh, the first baseman.

None of them seemed happy.

Great, Robbie thought. More teammates thrilled with my performance.

"Dude," Willie said sternly, "you're thinking too much."

Robbie nodded sheepishly. "Yeah," he said. "I tend to do that."

"Don't!" Connor said. "Just throw the ball over the plate."

"Yeah, try that," Willie said. "By the way, the plate is that white thing up there. In between the batter's boxes."

"The thing the ump keeps dusting off," Jordy added helpfully.

With that, the three looked at one another, rolled their

eyes, and trotted back to their positions.

"Thanks," Robbie murmured. "I feel much better now."

Actually, what he felt was a familiar tightening in his stomach, something that seemed to happen a lot lately when he pitched.

Okay, no thinking, he told himself. Just throw it.

Robbie got the sign from Joey again, wound up, and fired a fastball. It skipped in the dirt. Ball one. The next pitch, another fastball, was high. Ball two. Robbie could see that the kid at the plate wasn't going to help, either.

No, the kid was no dummy. He had learned his lesson. He wasn't swinging at any more junk out of the strike zone. Instead he stood there like a statue, bat on his shoulder, as Robbie skipped two more pitches in the dirt and the umpire cried, "Ball four!"

With a smirk, the kid tossed his bat aside and trotted down to first base.

The rest of the inning seemed to take forever.

Robbie walked the next batter on five pitches. He walked the batter after that on six pitches. Bases loaded. He was so nervous now, he was almost nauseated.

Oh, God, he thought, please don't let me hurl, too. I'm embarrassed enough without spewing in front of all these people.

But for the first time all game, the Orioles caught a break.

The next Tigers batter, a hulking kid named Ramon who Robbie recognized from gym class, swung at an outside pitch and looped a weak flare over second base. Willie and Yancy Arroyo, the Orioles center fielder, both gave chase.

For an instant, the ball looked like trouble. But Yancy called off Willie and made a running one-handed catch at the last second for the third out.

Robbie was never happier to get off the mound. Mike Cutko was scheduled to pitch the last two innings for the Orioles, which was fine with Robbie. He was done for the day—in more ways than one.

Oh, he was *so-o-o* done.

As he neared the dugout, his dad gave him a high five and said, "Way to get out of that jam." But Robbie knew his dad was just trying to be encouraging. Or maybe he felt guilty about riding his kid so hard.

Whatever, Robbie thought, the drive home should be fun. He pictured his dad with one meaty hand draped over the steering wheel, quiet and unsmiling, worried about whether he was doing a crappy job coaching the Orioles, and wondering why his kid was struggling so much with his control.

Taking a long swig from his water bottle, Robbie was struck by another thought: I wonder if it's too late to go out for lacrosse?

Robbie was slumped on the couch watching TV when he felt something bounce off the top of his head—*Boink! Boink!* He pretended to ignore it. Casually he reached for the remote.

Boink! Boink! There it was again. Robbie sighed. She won't go away, he thought. She never goes away. I know exactly what she wants, too.

Boink! Boink! He whipped his head around. Sure enough, there was his mom, smiling and holding out a Ping-Pong ball and two paddles as if they were weapons for a duel.

"You want to get schooled again?" she said. "Huh? Because I'll beat you like a rented mule."

Despite his lousy mood, Robbie couldn't help grinning. He had to give her credit: his mom was the best trash-talker in the whole world—better than any kid Robbie knew. Better than most pro athletes, for that matter.

Other kids' moms were friendly and talkative, sure. But there was no one like Mary Hammond. "Loud and proud," was how his dad described her. And she was wickedly funny when she trash-talked, too. Whenever Robbie's friends came over, she'd challenge them to one-on-one basketball in the driveway, or Wii games, or Monopoly— anything you could compete in. Most of the time his friends would be laughing so hard at her nonstop chatter that they could barely concentrate.

"You try being married to a cop and being Little Miss Demure," his mom once said of her personality. "Doesn't work. You'd get squashed like a bug."

His mom was no bug. She'd been a terrific athlete at the University of Maryland, a star second baseman on the softball team, and one of the best diggers the volley-ball team had ever had. Robbie had seen old grainy video of her laying out for ground balls and throwing herself around the polished volleyball court, and he wondered how she hadn't landed in the emergency room after every game.

She brought the same hard-charging mentality to everything she did in life, including her business: Catering by Mary ("Affordable Elegance for All Occasions"). Robbie feared that his mom's in-your-face attitude may have been what led his twin sister to go to boarding school this year. Though he would never admit it publicly, he missed hav-ing Jackie around the house—if only to divert some of his mom's attention.

"What's the matter?" she said, tossing Robbie a paddle. "Afraid to play me?" She flapped her arms as if they were wings. "Chicken? *Bawwk! Bawwk! Bawwk! Bawwk!*"

Robbie shook his head and laughed. "Okay, that does it," he said, clicking off the TV. "Your beat-down will be extra severe this time."

"Oooooh, now he's mad!" his mom said, rumpling his hair playfully. "I'm so sc-a-a-a-red!"

Seconds later they were bounding downstairs to the family room and the dark green Ping-Pong table, gleaming under the harsh fluorescent lighting.

"How was your game last night?" his mom asked as she straightened the net. "Sorry I missed it. Work is nuts. We've got three weddings this weekend. Did the Orioles finally win?"

Robbie groaned inwardly. For the past twenty-four hours he'd been doing everything he could to forget the game. Forget the final score: Tigers 6, Orioles 2. Forget the fact he couldn't hit the ocean—never mind the strike zone—with his pitches. Forget the growing feeling that he was letting down the team, and letting down his dad.

No, he didn't feel like getting into all that now.

"You wanna play, or you wanna talk?" he said, tossing the ball to his mom. "Your serve. Age before beauty."

She narrowed her eyes and pretended to be outraged. "Oh, now it's on!" she said. "You're going down."

But instead, Robbie quickly jumped out to a 10–5 lead. He was a strong all-around player with a good backhand— good enough to win his age-group championship at summer camp. But his mom was amazing at hitting the angles. And she had a tricky spin serve that made the ball shoot wildly off your paddle if you didn't adjust for it.

Plus, Robbie thought, she has that not-so-secret weapon: her mouth.

"You can't hold this lead!" his mom said as they volleyed furiously. "You'll crack like a three-minute egg!"

This time Robbie said nothing. His dad was right: the only way to beat his mom when she started trash-talking was to tune her out. "Pretend it's like static on the car radio," his dad always said. "Just ignore it."

But as the game went on, that was easier said than done. When he was leading 19–15, Robbie sailed two returns long and smacked his thigh in frustration.

"Aacckk!" his mom said, bugging out her eyes and wrapping both hands around her throat. "Is someone starting to choke? Someone need the Heimlich maneuver?"

But on the next point, she was the one who attempted a slam and sent it long. Robbie was at match point: 20–17. He looked at his mom. He could see the perspiration on her forehead. She was breathing hard too.

Again, he knew what was coming.

"Time-out!" she said, as if on cue. She put down her paddle and made a big show of elaborately fixing her ponytail.

"That's so lame, Mom," Robbie said, shaking his head.

"What?" she said innocently. "I'm not allowed to fix my hair?"

"Why don't you put some fresh lipstick on, too?" Robbie said. "Anyway, it won't work. You're just delaying the inevitable."

When she was finally ready, Robbie served. The two volleyed back and forth cautiously for a few seconds, each looking for an opening to attack. Finally, his mom slammed what looked to be a sure backhand winner on an impossible angle mid-table.

Except . . . somehow Robbie got to it.

He lunged to his right and hit an amazing forehand that

struck the top of the net. For an instant, the ball seemed to hover in the air. Then it dinked over for the winning point.

"NO-O-O-O!" his mother wailed, collapsing to the floor and laying facedown on the carpet.

Robbie shrugged and tossed his paddle on the table. "My work here is done," he said. He swiped a hand across his forehead. "Look at that. Didn't even work up a sweat."

"Oh, you're a cruel kid!" his mom said. She got to her feet and pretended to stagger over to the small refrigerator in the corner. She pulled out two water bottles and handed one to Robbie.

"This will haunt me forever," she said, plopping down on the sofa and running the cool bottle across her forehead. "I might never live it down."

Robbie sat and put an arm around her shoulder. "Don't worry," he said. "I won't tell anyone. Except Dad. And Jackie. And Ashley. And all my friends in school. And everyone on the Orioles."

His mom smiled wearily and blew a stray hair out of her face. "Speaking of the Orioles," she said, "tell me about the game."

Robbie frowned and pulled his arm away. "Didn't Dad already tell you about it?"

She turned to look at him. "Maybe I want to hear from the player's perspective."

"It was okay," he said with a shrug.

"That's it? 'Okay'?" his mom said. "Can we have a few details? Like maybe the score? And how my favorite son pitched?"

Robbie took a gulp of water. "Tigers beat us six–two,"

he said quietly. "Your favorite son gave up a lot of walks. Again."

"Yuck!" his mom said.

Robbie nodded. "I didn't even want to pitch. Not the way I've been going. But Dad says I have the best arm in the whole league."

"Not to mention lightning-fast reflexes," she said, gesturing toward the Ping-Pong table. "You just have to hang in there till your confidence comes back."

"You sound just like Dad."

"Who do you think coaches *him*?" his mom asked with a twinkle in her eye. "Seriously, he's right." She patted Robbie's hand. "You'll be back. You were always a great pitcher."

"Thanks for the use of the past tense," Robbie said morosely.

"Oh, you know what I mean," his mom said. She leaned over and kissed his forehead. For a moment, they sat in silence, sipping their water.

Finally his mom cleared her throat and said softly: "Do you still think about it? You know, what happened with Stevie?"

Robbie closed his eyes and felt a shiver go through him.

Do I still think about it?

Only every time I pick up a baseball.

He remembered it like it was yesterday: last summer's all-star game, Eddie Murray Field manicured and shimmering like a green oasis in the afternoon sunshine, the bleachers filled, Robbie Hammond on the mound for the South team, throwing serious heat.

He had mowed down the first two North batters with six straight fastballs, drawing low murmurs of approval from the crowd. The third batter managed a weak grounder to second and tossed his helmet in disgust. But that was just for show. Robbie could tell the kid was just grateful to make any kind of contact at all against a pitcher throwing seventy-plus miles per hour.

In the second inning, the North's cleanup hitter, a tall kid with dark hair and thick, muscular shoulders, strolled to the plate. Right away Robbie could tell there was something different about him.

The kid was chewing a big wad of bubble gum and seemed perfectly relaxed. There was no fear in his eyes. At the sight of him, the North parents and siblings all seemed to perk up, as if they were about to witness something special.

Maybe it was Robbie's imagination, but he seemed to remember the PA announcer giving the kid's introduction a little extra zing, too:

"NOW BATTING FOR THE NORTH ALL-STARS, NUM-BAH 12, STEE-VEE ALT-MANNNNN!"

The kid had stepped into the batter's box like he owned it. He took his time digging in, holding his right hand up and signaling the ump that he wasn't ready yet, the same way Derek Jeter of the New York Yankees always did.

Once he was set, he took three unhurried practice swings. Then he cocked his bat and looked serenely at Robbie as if to say: *Okay, it's showtime. Let's see what you got.*

Robbie was astounded. Will you look at this big jerk? he thought. Who does he think he is?

Instantly Robbie made a silent vow: This kid's going down. On three pitches. Just like the others.

But his first pitch to the kid, a nasty fastball, just missed inside for ball one. The kid made no attempt to swing. Instead he seemed to study the pitch with mild curiosity. Then he nodded to himself, stepped out of the batter's box, and took a few more easy swings.

Robbie's second pitch was even nastier, a missile that split the middle of the plate and smacked into the catcher's mitt with a loud *thwack!*

Again the kid stepped out and took a practice swing. And this time he calmly blew a huge bubble, as if he'd seen plenty of fastballs and those last two were no big deal.

Now Robbie could feel his irritation rising and the adrenaline pumping through him. The kid was playing games with him! Mocking him! Showing him up!

What is the *deal* with this guy? Robbie thought, gritting his teeth.

He went into a full windup, kicked high, and fired as hard as he could. Looking back on it now, it was probably the hardest pitch he had ever thrown in his life. But as soon as it left his hand, he knew something was terribly wrong.

Instead of heading for the outside part of the plate, the ball was tailing inside. *Way* inside. It kept tailing and tailing, as if in slow motion. In the next instant it plunked Stevie Altman square on the batting helmet, right above the left earflap. It sounded like a gunshot.

The boy went sprawling in the dirt. There was a gasp from the crowd. Then, for maybe five seconds, there was this awful silence.

He remembered seeing Stevie lying there, his right leg twitching, as both coaches jumped from the dugout and ran to him. A couple of dads rushed out of the stands, whipping out cell phones to call 9-1-1. One mom screamed. A knot of shaken North players hovered over their fallen teammate as the coaches shouted, "Move back! Give him room!"

Five minutes later an ambulance lurched to a stop beside the field, its siren wailing and lights flashing. Stevie's eyes were still closed when the paramedics lifted him on a stretcher, belted him in, and took him away.

Somehow Robbie had managed to finish the inning. He got the next two batters to chase bad pitches and hit weak ground balls to the second baseman. The third batter hit a foul pop to the first baseman. When the inning was over, Robbie walked back to the dugout in a daze. He barely seemed to notice when his coach put both hands on his shoulders and spoke to him in a low voice.

"It was an accident," the coach kept saying. "You didn't mean to do it. Shake it off, now."

A new pitcher took the mound for the South in the third inning, and Robbie watched the rest of the game from the bench. The South held on to win, 2–1. After the game, they handed out trophies to both teams. But Robbie, still thinking about Stevie, scarcely paid attention when the league commissioner congratulated him and handed him a gleaming gold trophy with a tiny figure of a batter on top.

That evening, Robbie and his dad had driven to the hospital to check on Stevie. Robbie dreaded seeing him— and his parents—but he knew it was the right thing to do. The Altmans met them in the lobby of the emergency room. Stevie had a concussion, they said. He was still being treated, and too groggy to talk to anyone. He would probably be kept in the hospital overnight for observation, they added. But the doctors were optimistic that he'd be all right. Stevie's mom thanked them for coming. Mr. Altman was quiet and calm, like Stevie had been in the batter's box.

Fifteen minutes later, Robbie and his dad were back in the car, headed home. Even though it was a warm summer night, Robbie felt a chill go through him. He asked his dad to roll up the windows.

"Robbie, I know you're upset," his dad had said. "But it's not like you beaned him on purpose. These things happen in baseball. It was just a pitch that got away. He'll be fine, you'll see."

But that hadn't made Robbie feel any better, either. He slumped in his seat as he recalled how angry he'd been when he pulled back his arm, then released the ball with all his might. . . .

And ever since that awful day, Robbie had struggled with his control every time he stepped on the mound. No matter what he did to try to fix the problem—and he'd tried lots of things—nothing seemed to work.

Now, here it was, a new baseball season, and still he thought often about Stevie.

No one seemed to know where Stevie was these days. Someone said the Altmans had moved out of town. Reportedly, Mrs. Altman had gotten a new job in a different state.

Robbie was relieved that he wouldn't have to face the kid again, but he was left with a lot of unanswered questions. He wondered if Stevie was okay, and if he was still playing baseball.

If he was, was he the same strong, confident batter as before?

Or did he flinch now every time the pitcher whipped his arm forward and the ball came spinning to the plate?

Did he get nervous and bail out on inside pitches? And when he closed his eyes at night, did he still see a fastball screaming at his head, ready to crash into his helmet and turn out the lights again?

Robbie's dad kept saying, "Be patient, son. Your control will come back. I know it will."

Maybe, Robbie thought. Or maybe not.

All he knew was this: he didn't want to hit another batter as long as he lived.

Marty Loopus pointed the video camera at Robbie and shouted, "Okay, we're rolling, and . . . ACTION!"

"This is the dumbest thing we've ever done," Robbie said, shaking his head.

It was a misty Saturday morning at Eddie Murray Field. Robbie was on the pitcher's mound, and Marty stood behind the chain-link backstop around home plate. He stared intently at the camera's LCD screen and gave the thumbs-up sign.

"Okay," he said. "Warm up first. A few easy throws."

"I don't know about this. . . ." Robbie said. He looked around uneasily and was glad that the park was nearly deserted. He only saw a couple of parents pushing their kids on the playground swings.

"This is gonna help you," Marty said. "Trust me."

Robbie sighed and grabbed a few baseballs from the bucket at his feet. He looked at the crude target Marty had fashioned on the backstop—four pieces of duct tape forming a square about the size of home plate—and tentatively lobbed a few balls at it.

Marty was Robbie's best friend on the Orioles—maybe his only friend, he thought wistfully. A skinny, nerdy-looking kid with thick glasses and flaming red hair, Marty was the team's right fielder and weakest player.

"No throw, no hit, no field," was the succinct way in which Willie described Marty's game. "Oh, and no run, too."

But Marty was also the smartest sixth-grader at York Middle School. It was rumored that he'd never gotten anything less than straight A's on his report card since the first grade.

The one time he had brought home a B-plus, back in fifth grade, his mom had jumped in the car that afternoon and driven to the school, demanding that the teacher recheck her son's test grades.

The teacher did and discovered a glaring error: she had marked down that Marty got an 85 on a big test when he had actually scored a 95. The teacher apologized profusely.

"That's okay, hon," Mrs. Loopus had said, patting the teacher's arm and flashing the icy smile of a Mafia don. "Just change the grade."

Which the teacher had done. And just like that, Marty's streak of academic perfection remained intact.

Okay, fine, Marty's a brainiac, Robbie thought now as he finished his warm-up tosses. But that doesn't mean this isn't a giant waste of time.

"Tell me again why we're doing this?" he said, hoping he didn't sound too whiny.

Marty lowered the camera and looked disbelievingly at his bud. "Didn't we go over this?" he said. "We're looking for flaws in your pitching mechanics. We're filming your windup and delivery. Then I'm sending it to my Uncle Moe, who works for the Orioles. The *major-league* Orioles, my skeptical friend. Uncle Moe thinks he can get the pitching coach to look at it. Maybe the coach can figure out why you have such a great arm and can't hit the broad side of a barn, as my dad says."

Seeing Robbie's face cloud over, Marty quickly added, "Um, no offense."

"There's no way a big-time Orioles coach would have time to look at a kid's video," Robbie said dismissively.

Marty wiped the mist from the camera lens with his sleeve and looked up again. "Well, then, there's another good reason for filming," he said. "To document your rise to glory from rag-armed Babe Ruth League hurler to over-powering big-league ace. Years from now, when you're a famous twenty-game winner and making millions and riding around in a limo, I'll sell this video to ESPN and make a fortune. Then I'll move into a ginormous mansion with servants and a big pool and my own ice cream truck out back." Marty smiled benevolently. "You can come hang out with me if you want."

"Gee, thanks," Robbie said. "Nice of you to include me."

"What are friends for?" Marty said cheerfully. He raised the camera again and said, "Okay, warm-ups are over. Now pitch like you would in a game."

Robbie frowned. "If I pitch like in a game," he said, "the ball might go over the backstop."

"Enough with the chitchat," Marty said, waving as the red RECORD light winked on. "Pop one in here. Aim for the target. Let's see how you look."

Robbie went into his windup, smooth and unhurried, just as his dad had taught him. He pivoted lightly on his right foot and brought his left knee up to his waist. Then he turned and fired, making sure to follow through all the way.

The ball smacked the middle of the target, sending a small cloud of dust in the air.

"Whoa!" Marty yelled. "Where did *that* come from? Bet it hit seventy on the radar gun, too!"

"I got lucky," Robbie said, reaching for another ball.

He went through his windup again, keeping it simple and compact, and fired. Again, the ball hit the target, caroming off the backstop with a loud *twwaanngg!*

Marty whooped, trying to keep the camera still, and shouted, "Look that that! Awesome! The boy's *all over* the plate today!"

"Trust me," Robbie muttered. "It won't last."

But it did—mostly. He threw eight more pitches and five hit the target. And the three that missed were off only by a couple of inches.

Finally, Marty grinned and waved. He turned off the camera and put it in his backpack.

"Okay, we're good," he said, jogging out to the mound. "That'll give the coach plenty to look at. But, dude, you were locked in! Nothing wrong with your control today."

He looked at Robbie intently and said, "How come you don't pitch like that in a game?"

It's a long story, Robbie thought. Which I don't feel like sharing just yet. Especially not with anyone on the Orioles. Even you, my geeky friend.

But all he said was, "That's what we're trying to find out, right?"

The two boys picked up their gloves and wandered into the outfield to play catch. The sky was beginning to clear and the sun was already peeking through the clouds, signaling a warm day. For forty-five minutes they threw towering fly balls to each other, laughing when they tried to make circus catches behind their backs and failed miserably. Which Marty did every time.

Then they practiced diving over the rickety fence in center field to snare home run shots, each boy providing the play-by-play call for the other:

"WELL HIT! THAT BALL COULD BE GONE! LOOPUS GOES BACK, BACK, BACK . . . NOW HE LEAPS AT THE WALL AND . . . I DON'T BELIEVE IT! HE ALMOST MAKES THE CATCH! WHAT AN EFFORT! UNBELIEVABLE! OH, THEY'LL BE SHOWING THAT ONE ON *SPORTSCENTER* TONIGHT, FOLKS, I GUARANTEE YOU!"

"THERE'S A SHOT TO DEEP CENTER . . . BUT HERE COMES HAMMOND! LOOK AT HIM FLY! HE MIGHT GET THERE! NOW HE REACHES UP AND . . . HE'S GOT IT! AND HE LANDS IN THE STANDS! LADIES AND GENTLEMEN, WE CAN ONLY HOPE HE'S ALL RIGHT! BUT WHAT AN AMAZING DISPLAY OF ATHLETIC TALENT!"

Finally, thirsty and tired and still chuckling, they drank from the water fountain and collapsed in the shade of a big maple tree.

But a moment later, Robbie grew serious. "Can I ask you something?" he said.

"Let me guess," Marty said. "You need help with math.

So you turn to one of the true geniuses of our time. I don't blame you. I'd do the same thing if I were of average intelligence."

Robbie rolled his eyes. "Well, at least you're modest about it," he said. "No, tell me something. What do the other kids on the team say about me? And don't worry about hurting my feelings. Be honest."

"They say you can't pitch," Marty said.

"Okay, maybe not that honest," Robbie said.

"They say you have a great arm," Marty continued. "But they think you're only pitching 'cause you're the coach's kid."

Robbie groaned. *The coach's kid.* He knew that one would come up sooner or later. He thought back to the day last April when Bill Howard, the league commissioner, had come over to the house and sat down with his dad at the kitchen table.

"Ray," Mr. Howard had said, "we don't have enough dads volunteering to coach. If a few don't step up soon, we won't have as many teams in the league this year. What a shame that would be for the kids."

Immediately, Ray Hammond had said, "I'll take a team." That's what cops did, pitch in. And that was his nature. When anyone needed a helping hand, Ray Hammond was the first to provide it.

He had never coached baseball before. But that didn't seem to matter.

The two men had stood and shook hands. And as his dad walked Mr. Howard to the door, Robbie had sat there with a sinking feeling. This won't make things any easier for me, he'd thought.

No, he'd seen it over the years with other boys whose dads coached their teams. Unless you were a superstar, kids always thought you were pitching or playing the infield only because your dad was in charge. They automatically assumed you were getting preferential treatment.

Now, listening to Marty, Robbie's worst fears were coming true. The other kids on the Orioles had seen him give up seven, eight walks a game, and they were thinking: My grandma could pitch better than that.

When he'd skipped balls in the dirt and sailed pitches over batters' heads, they'd thought: what's this scatter-armed loser doing on the mound for us?

He couldn't blame them, either. He sure wasn't helping the team right now.

"You didn't ask what I think," Marty said now.

"Huh?" Robbie said distractedly.

"You asked what the rest of the team was saying about you. But you didn't ask what *I* think."

Robbie sighed. He pulled a blade of grass from the ground and braced for the worst. Marty was not exactly Mr. Sensitive when it came to people's feelings.

"Go ahead," he said. "Tell me how much I suck."

"I think you're the best pitcher I ever saw," Marty said. "Well, for a kid, anyway. You're a natural. Your worst fastball is ten miles an hour faster than anyone else's. You'd have to be crazy not to see how much talent you have."

Robbie's jaw dropped.

"Once you've got control, there won't be anyone in the league who can touch you," Marty went on. "You'll strike out ten batters a game. I don't blame your dad for sticking with you. Besides, except for Mike, no one else on the team can pitch anyway."

Robbie studied Marty's face to see if he was putting him on. But Marty wore the same open, placid expression he always wore.

He's serious! Robbie thought. The realization filled him with relief. At least there was one Oriole who believed in him. Marty might be a little wack, but he was true blue.

Suddenly Marty stood and picked up his glove and backpack. "Okay, I gotta go," he said. "I'll have my dad run this video over to Uncle Moe today."

"You do that," Robbie said with a smile.

"In the meantime, don't stress so much about your pitching," Marty said. "Remember: 'There is no education like adversity.'"

"You just make that up?" Robbie said.

Marty shook his head. "Disraeli," he said. "You know, Benjamin Disraeli? The famous nineteenth-century British statesman?"

Robbie grinned and looked admiringly at his friend.

"Sure," he said. "Everyone knows that."

Coach Ray Hammond was grim-faced as he gathered the Orioles in the dugout. "Sit!" he said. Everyone sat. No one spoke. Robbie was afraid to move. He had never seen his dad so angry.

Moments earlier, the Orioles had lost 10–1 to the Red Sox. It was their eighth straight loss of the season. And this had been their ugliest loss yet—even more ugly than usual. Robbie watched his dad take off his cap and rub his hand wearily over his bristly scalp.

"Men," he said, "that was embarrassing. We played with no heart. No energy, either. I'm sick of it. I know you're sick of it, too. So we're not leaving until we figure out what the problem is. The floor is now open for suggestions." He folded his arms and gazed into the faces of his discouraged players.

For maybe ten seconds, no one spoke.

"The problem," Joey said finally, "is that we suck."

Coach Hammond pursed his lips and nodded. "Okay," he said, "that's a start. But could we be a little more specific?"

"We can't hit," Jordy said.

"We can't pitch, either," Robbie said quickly. Better to get that in before someone else does and the whole team mean-mugs me, he thought.

"Plus our fielding is horrible," Willie said. "How many errors did we have tonight? That was ridiculous."

The Orioles hung their heads and appeared lost in thought, as if each player was replaying this latest debacle in his mind.

Robbie thought back to his own three innings on the mound and cringed. This time he'd given up five runs on only six walks instead of seven. A sign of progress? Not really. Not when you skip about ten balls in the dirt and the Red Sox batters are doing the equivalent of a Mexican hat dance each time they come to the plate.

Somehow he had managed three strikeouts. Of course, all three came against the Red Sox number nine hitter, a chunky kid named Jonny Choobal who was willing to swing at anything and seemed relieved to quickly whiff and head back to the dugout where it was safe.

The Orioles bats had been quiet again too. Jordy and Connor had gotten the Orioles' only two hits. And Willie had scored their only run on a wild pitch by the Red Sox pitcher. By the fourth inning, the Red Sox had been openly mocking them, playing their outfielders so shallow it looked like a T-ball game.

"Pathetic," Robbie had murmured to himself when he spotted the Red Sox center fielder positioned about twenty feet behind the second baseman. It was the ultimate diss of the Orioles bats.

"So what are we going to do, men?" his dad said now,

pacing back and forth. "Now that we've determined that we stink—can't hit, can't pitch, blah, blah, blah—what are we going to do? Huh? Are we just going to throw up our hands and quit?"

For a moment the dugout was silent again, except for the occasional sound of spikes scraping the concrete floor.

"Well," Marty said at last, "there *is* a certain logic to quitting. Consider the avoidance of further pain and humiliation. The emotional rejuvenation that comes with disassociating oneself from a known stressor. The time spent in contemplation of other life goals one might achieve instead of baseball superiority."

Ray Hammond whirled and stomped over to where Marty sat. He leaned over and stuck his face inches from Marty's.

Hoo boy, Robbie thought, hope Dad brushed his teeth. Because his breath can be death after a slice of pepperoni pizza or a burger with onions.

"Marty," the coach said in a low growl, "we're not quitting."

"Yes, sir," Marty said, turning pale.

"And do you know *why* we're not quitting?"

Marty quickly shook his head.

"Because of the personal shame it would bring to each and every one of you young men," Robbie's dad said. "Because of the horrible precedent it would set: that it's okay to walk away from something each time you struggle in life. And because of the dishonor it would bring to the Orioles and the entire league."

He glared at Marty and said, "Do you understand?"

Marty gulped and nodded. "Yes, sir," he said. "Very logical. Totally agree."

"Good," Ray Hammond said, resuming his pacing. "So, if we're all in agreement that we're not quitting"—here he whirled around to see twelve heads bobbing up and down vigorously—"we need to find ways to be a better baseball team. Any ideas?"

The Orioles looked at each other and shrugged. Then Willie jumped to his feet.

Please, Robbie thought, don't make Dad go thermonuclear again.

"Coach," Willie said, "seems to me you have only two options. Number one, you could go out and get better players. But the rosters are set, so it's probably too late for that. Besides, where would you find a more charming group of young men than the one right here?"

He flashed a big smile and gestured grandly at his teammates. The rest of the Orioles chuckled nervously.

"Or, number two," Willie continued, "you could schedule an extra practice each week. We go back to working on the fundamentals, okay? We take extra batting practice, extra infield and outfield, too. And the pitchers can throw on the side between starts and work on their control."

He shot a withering look at Robbie and went on. "The idea is that we work our butts off. And pretty soon, just like in the movies, we go from being a bunch of lovable losers to being—ta-daaa!—a lean, mean, orange-and-black-wearing championship team! Okay, maybe I'm getting a little carried away. Maybe we don't win the championship. But we'd be a lot better than we are now."

With that, Willie took a seat again. The Orioles looked at Coach. They were relieved to see his stony features dissolve into a grin.

"Willie," he said, "you just might have something there. Yep, the more I think about it, the more I like it."

Willie jumped to his feet and bowed dramatically as the Orioles cracked up.

"Okay," Coach said when the laughter died down. "Willie's idea is great. We *do* need extra practice. But I want to apologize to you, too. Because, as your coach, I should have thought of that myself.

"As we all know, I'm new at this coaching business. And I know I've made mistakes. But I promise to work hard and earn your trust. Because I believe in you guys."

The Orioles let that sink in for a moment.

Then, in unison, they said: "Awwwww!"

Now it was Coach's turn to crack up.

"Fine, no more corny speeches," he said. "Practice at three o'clock tomorrow afternoon. Right here. Be ready to work hard. Let's see if we can't turn this season around."

Robbie watched his dad go down the bench high-fiving the Orioles, and the sight made him smile.

Sure, he thought, teams have big, dramatic turnarounds all the time in the movies. But do they actually have them in real life?

Then he remembered all the pitches he'd skipped in the dirt against the Red Sox, and all the runs he'd given up, and all the cold stares he'd gotten from his teammates.

That was real life right now.

And real life sucked.

"He's doing it again, Mom!" Ashley shouted.

Robbie shot her a death look and hissed, *"Shush!"* But Ashley was giggling too hard to pay any attention.

"He's making those weird faces!" she yelled. "Check it out!"

It was the next night and Robbie stood in front of the mirror in his bedroom. He was in his full Orioles uniform, including socks and spikes, with his cap pulled low over his eyes. For the past ten minutes he'd been practicing a scowl he hoped would make batters quake each time they stepped in against him.

The whole time he'd been under the impression that his door was locked. But somehow his sister had crept in undetected. Undetected, that is, until she started howling with laughter.

Aren't ten-year-old girls supposed to be noisy? he thought. This one moves around like a deer in the forest.

A particularly annoying deer.

"OUT!" he said, grabbing Ashley firmly by the shoulders

and pushing her toward the door. "You're in my personal space."

"Keep making those stupid faces," she said, "and you'll have all the personal space you want—permanently."

After ushering Ashley out of the room and making sure the lock was turned this time, Robbie shuffled wearily over to the computer and searched for *pitchers with control problems*. He was surprised to find dozens of stories, quite a few about major leaguers whose promising careers were cut short when they suddenly couldn't find the plate.

"Guess I'm not the only wacko with this issue," he muttered. "Just the only twelve-year-old wacko with it."

Practice that afternoon had started as a virtual repeat of the day Marty had filmed his delivery at the ball field. As long as Robbie threw on the sidelines to Joey, every pitch was around the strike zone. On many pitches Robbie was so dialed in Joey barely had to move his catcher's mitt. For Robbie, it felt like old times, the carefree days when he just reared back and threw hard and didn't worry about where the ball would go.

But the minute his dad asked him to throw batting practice, and a real, live kid stepped in against him, Robbie's control vanished—again.

It got so bad that, at one point, Connor watched six straight pitches go by without lifting the bat from his shoulder. The rest of the Orioles, bored out of their minds in the field, began hooting at Connor to swing.

"C'mon, C!" Willie had shouted. "Thought you were the big slugger on this team!"

"Maybe he's asleep!" Jordy had chimed in. "Either that

or he's doing his impersonation of an ice sculpture!"

"Can't swing when every pitch is three feet outside!" Connor had snapped, staring balefully at Robbie.

Robbie had felt his face redden and his stomach churn. Finally, on his eighth or ninth pitch to Connor, he managed to throw something hittable. But that was only because he took so much off his fastball it practically crawled to the plate. To no one's surprise, the big shortstop promptly smacked a towering drive over the left field fence, then looked at Robbie and said pointedly, "That's your fastball? That's *weak*."

After watching his son struggle with a few more batters, Ray Hammond had finally brought in Mike to pitch the rest of BP. Greatly relieved, Robbie had slunk off to right field to shag fly balls alongside Marty.

Now, bathed in the soft glow of the computer screen, Robbie grew more and more worried as he read about three big-league pitchers whose careers went up in flames when they couldn't throw strikes.

There was Rick Ankiel, the young phenom for the St. Louis Cardinals, who finished second in the National League Rookie of the Year voting in 2000. But in the playoffs that year, Ankiel suddenly lost his control and uncorked nine wild pitches in three games as the Cardinals lost the series to the New York Mets.

He was never the same after that. Finally his control was so erratic that he gave up pitching altogether and returned to the minor leagues to become an outfielder in the hope of someday getting back to the big leagues.

Before Ankiel there was Mark Wohlers of the Atlanta

Braves. Wohlers had a fearsome 103-mile-per-hour fastball and was one of the best closers in the majors. But in 1998 he suffered mysterious bout of wildness and walked thirty-three batters in twenty and one-third innings. Shortly after that he was sent down to the minors to play in obscurity.

Finally there was Steve Blass, a veteran pitcher with the Pittsburgh Pirates. After winning nineteen games in 1972, he, too, suddenly couldn't find the plate with his pitches. In 1973 he walked eighty-four batters in a little over eighty-eight innings and was out of baseball within two years.

In fact, Blass's struggles were so well documented that whenever a pitcher inexplicably lost the ability to throw strikes after that, the pitcher was said to have come down with "Steve Blass disease."

Reading this, Robbie thought: Great. With my luck, whenever some dopey kid starts sailing pitches all over the place, they'll call it "Robbie Hammond syndrome."

He logged off the computer and stared forlornly at the poster of Jim Johnson that dominated one wall. Johnson was Robbie's favorite pitcher on the big-league Orioles, a tall right-hander who could dominate opposing hitters with a fastball that routinely hit the mid-nineties on the radar gun.

How horrible would it be, Robbie thought, to have to give up pitching forever, just because you couldn't get the stupid ball over the plate? And would he, Robbie Hammond, be the first twelve-year-old in the whole wide world to ever experience such a fate?

Just thinking about it now made his hands sweat.

The truth was, Robbie loved everything about pitching—at least he *used* to love everything.

He loved how the pitcher was always the main focus of attention on a baseball diamond. He loved how the inning couldn't start until the pitcher went into his windup, just the way a concert couldn't start until the orchestra leader raised his baton.

He especially loved the feeling of standing on the mound and knowing he could locate a pitch anywhere he wanted and throw a fastball past any kid who dared step in against him.

I'd like to feel that again, he thought. Even one more time would be nice.

There was a knock at the door and his mom peeked her head in.

"Almost bedtime," she said. Then, seeing him in his Orioles uniform, she added, "Hey, those are some snazzy pajamas you got there. But I'd take the spikes off if I were you. They could be a little hard on my sheets."

Robbie managed a weak smile before she closed the door.

He looked in the mirror one last time and sighed.

If I could pitch the way I used to, he thought, I wouldn't have to practice these lame faces.

Once in bed Robbie found it hard to fall asleep. He tossed and turned for what seemed like an hour. Then, even though he wasn't supposed to, he grabbed his cell phone from the bedside table, turned it on under his sheets, and sent a quick text message:

Hey Marty. How's yr Uncle Moe? Give him my best ok?

The York Middle School cafeteria was crowded and noisy two days later when Marty plopped down into a seat across from Robbie and Joey. Robbie was glad to see him—until Marty reached into his backpack and pulled out a plastic container.

With great deliberation Marty opened the container and dumped the contents onto a paper plate.

Robbie and Joey stared at the brownish, pasty glop, which now emitted the overpowering odor of garlic.

"What . . . is . . . *that*?" Joey said finally.

"What's what?" asked Marty, who was now happily shoveling the goo into his mouth with a cracker.

"That . . . *stuff*," Joey said, pointing. "It looks like the mushed-up insides of a woodchuck."

"Smells like it, too," Robbie said.

"Oh, and by the way?" Joey said. "They have these new things now? For eating? They're called forks. You should try using one."

Marty paused only long enough to reach for another cracker. "For your information," he said, "this is baba ghanoush. It's eaten with crackers. Or pita bread. It's Egyptian."

"Egyptian," Joey repeated. "Like from Egypt?"

Marty shot him a pitying look. "This is why you'll go far, Joey," he said. "Yes, from Egypt."

Then Marty turned his full attention to Robbie. "So, ready to see a certain report card?"

Robbie looked nervously at Joey. "Well, I, uh—"

"Ugh," said Joey. "Don't you ever give it a rest, Marty? You can't go even one lunch period without bragging about your grades?"

"It's not that kind of report card," said Marty. "And it's none of your business." He pulled a paper out of his backpack. "This is something for my man Robbo here."

Robbie squirmed in his seat. "Um, Marty, why don't we do this some other time?" The last thing he wanted to do was talk about his problem in front of Joey.

Joey's eyes narrowed. "What, are you doing Robbie's homework for him now?"

"No, no, it's nothing like that," said Robbie quickly. "He's just, uh, giving me a little tutoring help in science. Isn't that right, Marty?" he added, sending a warning look to Marty.

"Oh, yeah, right," said Marty. He turned to Joey. "Want to join in the lesson? We're going to do a taste test experiment." And with that Marty brought the baba ghanoush right up to Joey's nose.

Joey made a face and tossed the rest of his cheeseburger on his plate. "Well, there goes my appetite," he said, gathering up his tray. "See you guys later. I'll know where to find you. In the nurse's office, getting your stomachs pumped."

"What's his problem?" Marty said as Joey hurried off. "Can't handle fine cuisine, I guess."

"Yeah, that must be it," Robbie said, feeling his own stomach getting queasy.

Marty shook his head and raked another cracker through the mushy mess. "Anyway," he said, "got Uncle Moe's report card on you, dude. But we can wait until later if you—"

"Give it here!" Robbie said, and he tried to snatch it out of Marty's hand.

"Patience, young man," Marty said, twisting so the paper was out of Robbie's reach. "I don't know if you're ready for the information contained herein."

"Just tell me what it says!" Robbie said through gritted teeth, looking around to make sure no one could hear. "And who wrote it?"

"As you know," Marty said, clearly enjoying keeping Robbie on pins and needles, "Uncle Moe works for the Orioles, in their front office. Like I promised—though you didn't believe it would happen—he got Rick Kranitz, their pitching coach, to look at your tape. And he e-mailed me Kranitz's comments."

"I can't believe it!" Robbie said, feeling an equal amount of excitement and dread. For an instant, he looked hopeful. But then his shoulders slumped again.

"Okay, go ahead," he said. "Tell me all the things I do wrong."

Marty made a big show of unfolding and smoothing out the paper. "Actually," he said finally, "Kranitz said there's nothing wrong with your pitching mechanics. In fact, he called your delivery"—here he held up the e-mail and began reading—"'a symphony of motion for a young kid.'"

Robbie regarded him suspiciously. "Are you messing with me?"

"Nope," Marty said. "And there's more. 'Leg kick appears smooth. Weight transfer during windup is good. Good shoulder turn and stride. Release point is excellent. Love the way he follows through and ends up perfectly balanced to field his position.'"

Robbie was stunned.

"He said all that?"

"He did," Marty said, handing him the printout. "Check it out yourself."

Robbie read the two neatly typed paragraphs. Then he read them again to make sure he didn't miss anything.

"So that's good news, right?" Marty said.

"Yeah, I . . . *guess*," Robbie said, nodding uncertainly.

"Try not to look so overjoyed," Marty said. "Yeah, we know you have control problems. But at least now we know your pitching fundamentals are sound. So it's not that."

He munched on another cracker and looked thoughtful. "And if it's not that," he continued, "what could it be?"

Robbie shrugged. Neither boy said anything for several seconds.

Suddenly Robbie blurted, "I guess it's all in my head. Maybe it's something that happened a while ago and it's still bothering me. Who knows how the brain works, right? Sometimes you try and try and try to fix something. Only the harder you try . . ."

His voice trailed off. He looked down at his hands and noticed they were shaking slightly.

Marty pushed his plate aside and studied his friend for a moment.

Finally he said, "Is there something you're not telling me?"

Robbie started to answer, but just then the bell rang for sixth period.

"Okay," Marty said as they gathered up their lunch bags, "we'll save that for another time. But don't stress, dude. You'll start throwing strikes again. Remember what Shakespeare said."

Robbie looked at him blankly.

"'How poor are they that have not patience! What wound did ever heal but by degrees?'"

"Sure," Robbie said, "easy for him to say. He never walked twenty-seven batters in fifteen innings like I did."

"Okay, you got me there," Marty said. "Shakespeare wasn't much of a baller. Decent writer, but probably a total rag-arm on the mound."

Robbie managed a weak grin.

"Right now," he said, "I kinda know the feeling."

It was a warm, sunny afternoon at Eddie Murray Field, and the Orioles were getting ready to play the Blue Jays. It was the game they had looked forward to all week.

"Perfect day for the Loser Bowl!" Willie said as they warmed up. "Are they carrying this on ESPN?"

The Orioles were calling it the Loser Bowl because the Blue Jays were also winless. In fact, it was rumored that the Jays were every bit as bad a baseball team as the Orioles—possibly even worse, which was hard for the Orioles to fathom.

At the moment, most of them were lined up along the fence in shallow left field, watching the Jays take infield.

"Know what? These guys *are* terrible," Connor said as a ground ball went through the third baseman's legs and the kid slammed his glove in frustration.

"I thought we were bad," Jordy said. "They make us look like all-stars."

Watching the Blue Jays shortstop boot yet another easy grounder, Willie shook his head in wonder.

"I want everyone to hear this," he said, raising his hands for quiet. "If we lose to these guys, I'm quitting this game. Forever. I'm dead serious, too. I'll join the swim team. I'll play in the band. But I will never, ever be seen in a baseball uniform again if these guys beat us."

The rest of the Orioles nodded solemnly and continued watching with fascination.

Just then, the Blue Jays coach yelled "Bunt!" and tapped the ball a few feet in front of home plate.

The hulking Jays catcher whipped off his mask, lumbered after the ball, and promptly tripped over it. Finally retrieving it, he fired it ten feet over the first baseman's head.

"Oh . . . my . . . God!" Jordy whispered, eyes widening.

"Is this, like, some kind of new reality series?" Mike said. "Like they're following around the worst youth team ever assembled? And we just can't see the TV cameras?"

Watching his first baseman run after the errant throw, the Jays coach wore a pained expression.

"Stand back! Their coach looks like he's gonna hurl!" Willie whispered now as the rest of the Orioles cracked up.

Warming up with Joey farther down the sideline, Robbie found himself feeling cautiously optimistic for the first time all season.

Part of that had to do with the crappy Blue Jays hitters he knew he'd be facing. "Who needs to pitch against a bad team more than I do?" he murmured.

But he was also buoyed by the fact that, just twenty minutes before game time, his fastball was going exactly where he wanted it to go. And just like in the old days, it was slamming into Joey's glove hard enough to rock the big catcher back on his heels.

On every fifth pitch, just to mix things up, Robbie would throw a changeup. Or he'd snap off a curveball that dropped viciously at the last minute, leaving Joey to dive to his knees and dig the ball out of the grass.

When the two were finished, Joey gave a low, appreciative whistle. "You're in the zone today, bro!" he said. "Just in time to get our first win!"

Maybe, Robbie thought, smiling wanly. Too bad we actually have to play the game with batters. If it was just me throwing to Joey, I'd look like a Player of the Year candidate every time.

A moment later, he watched his dad walk toward him with a strange look on his face.

"Robbie . . ." his dad began, head down.

The last time Robbie had seen that look, Ray Hammond had summoned his family into the living room to tell them his raise at the police department had fallen through and they wouldn't be going to Disney World after all.

Whatever's coming, Robbie thought, it won't be good news.

It wasn't.

"Mike's going to start for us," his dad said quietly. "He'll probably pitch the whole game, too. Just to give you a little break. Help clear your mind."

Robbie was speechless but not surprised. For the past couple of weeks, he'd been dreading the possibility of his dad making a pitching change. After all, even on a pitching-poor team, how could the Orioles keep trotting out a kid who couldn't find the plate and kept making opposing batters dance with all his wild fastballs in the dirt?

Still, now that the moment had actually arrived, it was killing him. He wished he had shared Kranitz's report with his dad. But he'd been afraid to. He didn't want his father thinking Robbie was going behind his back to get better coaching advice.

Robbie rubbed his eyes. No tears, he told himself. That's all I need the guys to see: me blubbering like a baby.

"Yancy's not feeling well," his dad continued. "So you're playing center field."

Robbie nodded numbly. His dad draped an arm around his shoulder and gave a reassuring squeeze. "This'll be a good change of pace for you, son." Then to Joey he said, "Go warm up Mike."

The Blue Jays pitcher was a tall kid with freckles whom the Orioles promptly nicknamed Spots. Watching him warm up at the start of the game, the Orioles saw that he seemed to have only two speeds: slow and slower.

Leaning on his bat in the on-deck circle, Willie was practically salivating at the prospect of facing one of Spots's nonexistent fastballs. "We're going to kill this guy," he muttered.

The rest of the Orioles nodded in agreement. Joey and Jordy, their number two and number three hitters, were so eager to hit that they were already wearing their batting helmets and taking practice swings at the far end of the dugout.

But somehow Spots made it out of the first inning unscathed. Willie swung viciously at the first pitch and lifted a fly ball to the third baseman for the first out. Joey swung just as hard and topped a slow roller to the second baseman, who gloved this one smoothly and threw to first for the second out. And Jordy, swinging for the fences, got under a pitch and hit a routine fly ball to center.

Just like that, it was side retired in order.

Bounding off the mound, Spots smiled and gave a little fist pump.

"Look at that fool!" Willie hissed. "Like he's Roy Halladay and he just punched out the side in the World Series!"

Trotting out to center field instead of jogging a few feet to the pitcher's mound between innings seemed weird to Robbie. He felt a million miles away from the action. He yawned and looked around. How does anyone stay awake out here? he wondered.

But Mike retired the Blue Jays in order, striking out their leadoff hitter and getting the next two batters to hit weak comebackers to the mound. The Orioles hustled off the field.

Before heading out to coach third base, Robbie's dad called them together. "Men," he said, "I have an important announcement before we bat. Babe Ruth is dead."

The Orioles exchanged puzzled looks. Then Marty brightened.

"That's right!" he said. "He died August 16, 1948. At age fifty-three. From throat cancer, I believe."

"Thank you, Mr. Human Wikipedia," Coach said dryly. "The point is, you're all swinging like the Babe. You're all trying to kill the ball. I know you're champing at the bit to hit one off this guy, but be patient up there. Short, compact swing. Just drive the ball."

But again the Orioles went down in order against Spots. Connor flied out to left, and Carlos Molina, the third baseman, hit a weak line drive to the shortstop. Riley Adams, the left fielder, popped out to the catcher and tossed his bat in frustration.

"There's that stupid fist pump again!" Willie said, watching Spots celebrate. "Do you realize how embarrassing this is?"

Fortunately, Mike kept the Blue Jays batting order off balance too. Both pitchers scattered four hits apiece over the next three innings as the game settled into a pitcher's duel.

Finally, with one out in the top of the sixth, Connor doubled into the gap in left-center field and Carlos walked. The Orioles dugout stirred. For the first time all game, the smile was gone from Spots's face, replaced by a bewildered frown.

"This is it!" Marty said. "He's getting tired!"

Jordy snorted. "How can you tell?" he said. "What, his fastball goes from fifteen miles per hour to ten?"

Riley followed with another walk to load the bases. And as Spots kicked the dirt in frustration, the Orioles came to life.

In the on-deck circle, Robbie knocked the doughnut off his bat and made his way to the plate. He had always been a pretty good hitter, and now he was surprised at how calm he felt.

"Level swing!" his dad shouted. Robbie took a couple of

practice cuts, then dug in and took a deep breath. Purposely he avoided looking out at Spots until the very last second. When he did, he was surprised to see how nervous the Blue Jays pitcher looked.

Boy, do I know *that* feeling, Robbie thought grimly. For an instant, he even felt sorry for the kid.

But there was no time for that, because Spots's first pitch was on its way, a tantalizing, chest-high floater that almost seemed to stop midway to the plate. Robbie's eyes widened. It looked the size of a beach ball.

Wait for it, wait for it, he told himself. Then he turned his shoulders perfectly and flicked the bat, ripping a double down the left field line that scored Connor and Carlos as Riley took third.

The Orioles dugout exploded with noise. When Robbie pulled into second base, he saw that his teammates were on their feet, banging their bats on the bench and pointing at him and cheering.

He realized it was the first time all season that his teammates actually looked happy over something he did.

That was it for Spots. The Blue Jays manager popped out of the dugout. A minute later Spots was trudging disconsolately off the mound and a new pitcher was warming for the Jays. The new kid had a decent fastball, striking out Mike and getting Marty on a one-hopper to first to end the inning.

Hustling in to get his glove, Robbie saw that the mood in the dugout was electric now. The Orioles led 2–0. And after all these weeks of losing, their first win was in sight.

If they could just hold on for one more inning . . .

"Three more outs!" Willie shouted, running the length of the bench and slapping hands with his excited teammates. "That's all we need! Three outs!"

Just then, Ray Hammond clambered down the dugout steps.

"Robbie," he said, "get loose. You're relieving Mike."

With that, the Orioles fell silent.

Robbie's heart pounded as the first Blue Jays batter stepped in against him.

Thanks for the heads-up, Dad, he thought. What did I get, a whole nine pitches to warm up?

Then he realized his dad probably did him a favor by waiting until the last minute to tell him he was relieving Mike. That was the smart thing to do with wacko pitchers who couldn't throw strikes. Don't give them too much time to think. Just run them into the game. And hope they throw the ball near the plate and get someone out.

Not that there's any pressure on me, he thought. He looked over at the Orioles' cheering section, which was into the game for the first time all season. Then he turned and checked out his amped-up teammates, who were on their toes and pounding their gloves and hollering encouragement.

No, he thought, all I have to do is close out our first win—maybe our only win of the whole season.

Or else everyone on the team will hate me forever.

"Time!" Joey said suddenly and shuffled out to the mound.

"You okay?" he asked. "You look like you're gonna faint."

"I look that good, huh?" Robbie said. He managed a weak grin. "I'm okay. Just a little nervous, is all."

Joey nodded. "Okay," he said, "we'll make it easy on you. If I put down one finger, you throw the fastball. If I put down two fingers, you throw the fastball. If I put down three fingers—"

"Let me guess," Robbie said. "Fastball?"

"Correct," Joey said. "Just throw like you did before the game. Fire it in there. Don't worry about anything. Remember, this is the Loser Bowl. No Babe Ruths in their lineup either."

As Joey shuffled away, Robbie shook his head in amazement. Joey was possibly the dumbest kid he'd ever known. But he was a great catcher. And every once in a while the big guy was capable of uttering simple truths that could both calm and inspire his teammates.

He's right, Robbie thought. *No Babe Ruths in that lineup.* What's there to worry about?

Just the usual stuff, it turned out.

He walked the first Blue Jays batter on four balls. He walked the second on five balls. Now he could feel his face getting hot and the sweat starting to trickle down his cheeks. Here we go again, he thought. He realized he was squeezing the ball so hard his hand ached.

Luckily, the Orioles caught a break when the third Blue Jays batter swung at a pitch a foot off the plate and hit a weak dribbler to Jordy for the first out as the runners moved up.

"How could you swing at that?!" Robbie heard the Blue Jays coach say as the kid slunk back to the dugout. "Their pitcher just threw nine straight balls! Don't help him out!"

Robbie suppressed a smile and thought: Leave him alone, Coach. Heck, that kid's got my vote for MVP of the game.

"TWO MORE OUTS!" Willie shouted, and now the rest of the Orioles took up the chant: "TWO MORE OUTS! TWO MORE OUTS!"

Like it could ever be that easy, Robbie thought.

Somehow he managed to get two quick strikes on the next batter, who wasn't about to swing after the tongue-lashing his teammate had just received. But Robbie followed that with four straight balls outside, and the batter trotted down to first as the Blue Jays dugout erupted.

Bases loaded.

Winning run on first base.

"TIME!" a voice cried. Ray Hammond popped out of the Orioles dugout. When he reached the mound, his voice was surprisingly gentle.

"How do you feel?" he asked.

"Oh, you know," Robbie said, wiping his face with his sleeve. "I've been better."

His dad grunted. He took the ball and rubbed it up with both hands for several seconds, looking thoughtfully at his son. Then he handed the ball back and said, "I know you can do this. But *you* have to know you can do it."

With that he turned and walked slowly back to the dugout.

Out of the corner of his eye, Robbie could see his teammates glancing at each other uneasily.

"Two more outs!" Willie shouted again. But he sounded tentative now. And Robbie noticed the chatter behind him had decreased noticeably in volume.

Robbie was pitching tentatively, too, almost trying to will the ball over the plate now. He took so much off his fastball that the next batter promptly slapped a single to right that drove in two runs.

Tie score: Orioles 2, Blue Jays 2. The noise from the Jays dugout was deafening. It grew even louder moments later when, still trying to aim the ball, Robbie walked the next batter on five pitches.

Bases loaded.

Again.

Winning run just sixty feet away.

Now Robbie was furious with himself. He slammed the ball into his glove and stalked around the mound. That'll never happen again, he vowed. If I get beat, I get beat. But it's going to be with my best stuff.

He was still seething when the next Blue Jays batter dug in. Robbie's first pitch was a fastball right down the heart of the plate. The kid took a big swing. But there was no catching up to this kind of heat, not with Robbie this pumped.

Strike one.

The next pitch was another missile that the kid missed by a mile.

Strike two.

Behind him, the Orioles' hopes began to flicker again.

This was the hardest they'd seen Robbie throw all season. At least for right now, he looked like a completely different pitcher from the jittery kid with flop sweat who had started the inning.

Now Robbie wasted a couple of fastballs outside, hoping the kid would chase a bad pitch. Didn't happen. The kid didn't swing at the next pitch, either, which just missed low and away.

Now the count was full. Robbie stared in at the batter and murmured, "You have no chance to hit this. None."

He kicked and fired another missile, maybe his fastest pitch yet. The kid held up again. But the pitch appeared to catch the outside corner of the plate.

For an instant, the crowd seemed to hold its breath. So did the Orioles. Robbie leaped in the air.

Come on, ump! he pleaded silently. Ring him up! Stee-rike three!

But the umpire's right hand didn't move.

"BALL FOUR!" he said. And now the runner on third was smiling and bounding to the plate with his hands raised in triumph as the Blue Jays poured out of their dugout to celebrate.

Game over.

Final score: Blue Jays 3, Orioles 2.

Robbie walked off the mound in a fog. He was still in a fog as the two teams lined up and slapped hands, the Blue Jays whooping and laughing, the Orioles stunned and downcast.

A dozen thoughts raced through his mind. It was all so unbelievable! They were the losers of the Loser Bowl. How bad did you have to be to do that?

And to lose to the freaking Blue Jays! And all because he blew a two-run lead. No, his teammates would never let him forget this one. They'd never forgive how he let them down.

And what about Willie? Was the little guy serious about quitting baseball forever now that the Orioles had lost to the worst team in the league? That'll be my legacy, Robbie thought sadly. *Psycho kid pitcher causes teammate to quit the game he loves.*

He watched as the rest of the Orioles silently gathered up their equipment and trudged off, some of them turning to look at him and shake their heads sadly.

He felt a hand on his shoulder. Looking up, he saw it was his dad. "That was a tough call," Coach Hammond said quietly. Now someone else was at his side too. It was Marty, telling him not to worry, it was just one game, he was still a great pitcher, he just had to work on a few things and everything would be fine.

But Robbie didn't feel fine.

He thought he was going to be sick.

The carnival was a jumble of bright lights, loud noises, and exotic smells as Robbie and Marty walked along the packed midway and stared up at the giant spinning Ferris wheel illuminated against the night sky.

It was five days after the Blue Jays game and the Orioles were visiting the carnival as a team. They were even wearing their uniform jerseys. The whole thing was Coach Hammond's idea.

"It'll be fun," he had explained to the Orioles at their last practice. "Something we can all do together. You know, to promote team unity."

"Team unity," Robbie chuckled to himself now. "That's a good one."

From the moment they had walked through the front gate, most of the Orioles had made it clear they had no intention of hanging out with one particular teammate, a certain short, squat, wild-throwing coach's kid who was killing them on the mound.

Each time Robbie tried to join a conversation, the other guys ignored him. And they made sure to walk far enough ahead of him to limit mingling. Even Joey seemed eager to avoid him.

The only one hanging with Robbie now was Marty— good ol' Marty, he thought gratefully, as faithful as a Labrador retriever. Bringing up the rear of this Orioles posse, with their arms around each other's waists, were Robbie's mom and dad, serving as the dutiful, if clueless, chaperones.

"Isn't this great?" his dad said. "I think the team's really enjoying this outing."

"Oh, it's great, all right," Robbie said, looking at Marty and rolling his eyes.

"Let me know if anyone wants to get owned in that basketball game," Mary Hammond said, smiling. "You know, where you shoot the big ball through the tiny hoop? I'm a whiz at that."

"Okay, Mom," Robbie said, grabbing Marty by the shoulder and steering him to the food booths. "Uh, we're gonna get something to eat. We'll catch up to you."

The two boys wandered through a maze of vendors selling fried dough, french fries, funnel cakes, sausage and peppers, barbecue chicken, pulled pork sandwiches, and much more. Finally, Robbie stopped at a booth covered with red, white, and blue bunting.

"A corn dog, dude?" Marty said. "Seriously? That's what you're eating?"

"Oh, listen to Mr. Weird Food Lover," Robbie said. "What are you having? Hummus-on-a-stick?"

Marty sighed and shook his head. "Robbie, Robbie, Robbie . . . I'm disappointed in you," he said. "Fine, go ahead and get your corn dog. With its suspect ingredients. And bland cornmeal batter. And ho-hum taste. Then meet me at that table over there. Be right back."

Robbie sat happily devouring his treat until his friend returned a few minutes later clutching a Styrofoam container. He opened it to reveal a thin whitish slab of *something*—Pork? Chicken? It was hard to tell—topped with what appeared to be herbs and spices.

Robbie stared at it for several seconds. "Okay," he said at last, "you got me. What *is* that?"

Marty beamed and tore off a piece and popped it in his mouth. "Catfish," he said between bites. "They wanted to deep-fry it, of course. It's practically the law at carnivals, right? Everything has to be deep fried? Except I told 'em mine had to be broiled."

Robbie was incredulous. "*Catfish*, Marty?" he said. "What are you, fifty years old? What kid goes to the carnival to eat catfish?"

"A worldly and discerning one, dude," Marty said, munching away. "A kid far more intelligent and mature than his peers. I know that hurts. But deal with it."

They finished eating and quickly caught up to the rest of the Orioles. Robbie sighed as he watched them stop to shoot baskets at the tiny hoops, his mom shooting along with them and trash-talking nonstop.

"Don't let it bother you," Marty said.

"Don't let what bother me?"

"The juvenile antics of certain people," Marty said, nodding at his teammates. "You don't want to hang with them anyway. Not when they're calling you . . . no, never mind."

Robbie turned to look at him. "When they're calling me *what?*"

Marty pretended to zip his mouth shut. "My bad," he said. "Forget it. Should have never brought it up."

Robbie narrowed his eyes and said, "If you don't tell me, I'll strangle you. Right here. In front of all these people. Think about it: you'll never eat catfish at the carnival again."

Marty gulped and looked away. "Well, if you're going to get an attitude . . ." he said. "But it's not nice, what they're calling you. Might be too much for a kid to handle. You could be in therapy for years."

"If you don't tell me," Robbie growled, "I'll be in prison for years. For murdering you."

"Fine," Marty said with a shrug. "Their new nickname for you is Ball Four."

Robbie winced and gazed over at his teammates, laughing and high-fiving as they launched shots at the absurdly tiny hoops.

"Okay, that one hurts," he said. "Guess you can't blame them. I've definitely thrown a lot of ball fours."

Marty nodded sympathetically and clapped a hand on his friend's shoulder. "Just leave me out of it when you talk with the therapist," he said.

For the next forty-five minutes, the Orioles wandered the midway playing whatever games they came across: the water gun race, the ring toss around the rubber duckie, the softball toss into ten-gallon milk cans, etc.

Finally they arrived at the baseball throw. It consisted of a canvas backdrop painted with a cheesy image of a batter standing menacingly at home plate with his bat cocked. Behind him crouched a catcher offering a target with his upraised mitt. The object was to throw the ball into a hole cut in the mitt.

When he spotted the Orioles in their jerseys, the grizzled old man working the booth seemed to light up.

"WHAT DO WE HAVE HERE?" he said in a booming voice. "A GEN-U-INE BASEBALL TEAM? STEP RIGHT UP, FELLAS! THREE THROWS FOR A DOLLAR. ONE BALL IN THE HOLE WINS A PRIZE!"

Robbie and Marty hung back. One by one, the rest of the Orioles stepped up to test their skill. Willie, Jordy, and Connor, the players with the best arms on the team, watched their throws sail high and bang harmlessly into the canvas. Joey, Yancy, and Gabe slowed down their throws and saw them land too low. Mike tried aiming his throw as if he were tossing a dart at a dartboard, earning hoots of derision from his teammates.

No one even came close to hitting the hole.

"Game's a rip-off, man," Willie grumbled.

"Yeah," Jordy said. "Look how small that hole is!"

Hearing this, the old guy cackled. "ONE IN IS ALL IT TAKES!" he cried. "WHO'S GONNA BE OUR FIRST WIN-NAH?"

He pointed a bony finger in Robbie's direction and shouted, "YOU THERE! YOU LOOK LIKE A PITCHER! STEP RIGHT UP, SON! LET'S SEE WHAT YOU CAN DO!"

Robbie froze and glanced around. Everyone was staring at him. He spotted his mom and dad looking on with bemused smiles.

"Me?" Robbie said. "Oh, no, I . . . no, thanks."

He started to walk away.

Then he heard it.

"No, not ol' Ball Four," Willie cracked. "He'd be low and outside every time."

Robbie stopped dead in his tracks as the rest of the Orioles snickered. He turned slowly and stared hard at Willie. Then he walked up to the old man, pulled a dollar from his pocket, and tossed it on the counter.

"Three, please," Robbie said.

When the balls were put in front of him, he paused to stare at Willie again. Then he fired one ball after another at the target—*WHAM! WHAM! WHAM!*—seemingly without aiming.

All three balls shot cleanly through the hole.

As Marty whooped, the rest of the Orioles gaped in astonishment. The old man gave an appreciative whistle and handed Robbie a small, purple stuffed monkey.

"LOOK AT THAT!" the old man bellowed. "SEE HOW EASY IT IS, FOLKS? STEP RIGHT UP NOW! WHO'S NEXT?"

Robbie turned to leave, but Willie stepped in front of him.

"You're so freakin' lucky," he said in a low voice. "You couldn't do that again in a million years."

Robbie smiled grimly and nodded. "Somehow, I knew you'd say that," he said. He fished another dollar from his pocket and held up three fingers. The old man happily handed him the balls.

Robbie shot one last look at Willie. Then he turned and threw all three balls even harder than the first time.

Again, all three found the hole.

From behind him, he could hear his mom and dad cheer and Marty cry, "That's my man!" When Robbie turned around, he saw that the rest of the Orioles looked stunned.

"FOLKS, MAYBE WE MADE THIS GAME *TOO* EASY!" the old man shouted. "STEP RIGHT UP! ONE IN MEANS A WIN! IF THE BOY HERE CAN DO IT, SO CAN YOU!"

From behind the counter, he pulled out a yellow stuffed giraffe. It was much bigger than the purple stuffed monkey. But Robbie waved him off.

"I'm not through yet," he said firmly. He handed the old man another dollar and said, "Three more, please."

By now a crowd had gathered, and the rest of the Orioles, buzzing with excitement, were pressed in around Robbie. This time, he took the three balls and backed up until he was ten feet farther from the target.

"No way!" Willie said. "From that far away? That's crazy!"

"If you say so," Robbie said calmly.

He looked up at the night sky and saw that the stars had come out. He took a deep breath and looked down again, eyes locked on the target. Now he went into a full windup, turned, kicked, and fired. *WHAM!*

The ball disappeared into the hole.

He went through the same routine two more times— *WHAM! WHAM!*—making sure to follow through the way he would in a game.

Each time, the ball shot through the hole.

Now the Orioles erupted, cheering and high-fiving each other and clapping him on the back. The old man looked irritated. From the top shelf of the booth, he pulled down a giant stuffed panda bear and shoved it at Robbie.

"Kid," he muttered, "I've been doing this for twenty-five years. Never seen nothin' like what you just did."

Robbie smiled and gave the thumbs-up sign to his mom and dad. With the Orioles chanting, "ROB-BIE! ROB-BIE!" he held the panda over his head, as if it were a championship trophy.

He went over to Willie, who still appeared to be in shock.

"Here," Robbie said, thrusting the panda in his arms. "A little present from Ball Four. Hope you enjoy it."

Then he turned and walked away, with Marty running after him.

Robbie couldn't concentrate in school

on Monday. In math class that morning he found himself gazing out the window and reliving the crazy events of the past forty-eight hours.

It seemed as if half the kids at York Middle had heard about his little throwing exhibition at the carnival. The minute he walked through the double doors, students were rushing up to congratulate him and request a play-by-play of the feat. A few had even asked for his autograph! Just before Homeroom he had run into Marty, who was wriggling like a puppy with excitement.

"Dude, you're a living legend!" Marty had said. "Everyone's talking about that golden arm of yours!"

"Too bad I'm not legendary where it counts—on the mound," Robbie said, tossing his backpack in his locker. "And how did everyone find out, anyway?" He narrowed his eyes and gazed suspiciously at Marty. "Has a certain big-mouth bud of mine been telling the entire world?"

"Not me," Marty said. "I swear. It's everyone else on the team. Especially Connor and Jordy. Willie, too, if you can believe it. They're talking you up, big-time."

"Even Willie?" Robbie said. "Amazing. How's he like that big panda?"

"Dude, he brought it to school!" Marty said.

"Wha—? You gotta be kidding me!"

The memory of that conversation made Robbie smile now. But it also made him wonder how a kid who can pump nine straight balls into a tiny hole could not be able to blow away batters.

"Yeah, how?" he heard himself say.

Suddenly another voice, deeper and richer, said, "*How*, Mr. Hammond? Whatever do you mean?"

With a start, Robbie realized he'd been daydreaming. Looking around sheepishly, he saw the entire class staring back at him. The teacher, Mr. Rumsey, a tall, distinguished-looking man in a white oxford shirt, sports jacket, and red bow tie, stood in the front of the classroom, an amused look on his face.

"Ladies and gentlemen," Mr. Rumsey said, "by the look of things, Mr. Hammond has not been with us for the past few minutes. At least not mentally. Possibly he has been on another planet. Or he has been thinking about a pretty young lady. Or baseball. Or his favorite video game. Anything to escape the incredible, all-encompassing tedium that is mathematics."

The other students chuckled. Robbie felt his face redden.

"How do I know Mr. Hammond has been elsewhere mentally?" Mr. Rumsey continued, pacing back and forth in front of the blackboard. "Simple: because he was smiling. You see, my students don't smile. No, my students come to class each and every day with the same cheerful demeanor as prisoners about to face a firing squad."

Now everyone in the class was giggling. Mr. R. was on a roll. The students had seen this kind of self-deprecating performance from their teacher many times before. And it was always hugely entertaining.

"Yes, I am the single most boring teacher in the history of York Middle School," Mr. Rumsey continued, his voice rising. "So it's little wonder our young friend here zoned out earlier. And you can bet he will zone out quite a few more times before this semester is over.

"And do you know why? Because the sound of my voice is more effective than any sleep aid on Earth. Why, even now, as I listen to myself prattle on and on, I can almost feel myself slipping into a deep slumber."

He paused in the center of the classroom. Raising his arms, he looked beseechingly at the class. "Ladies and gentlemen," he said, his voice a stage whisper, "I'll admit it. As an educator, I am a fraud. A complete and utter failure."

By this time the whole class was laughing uproariously. Even Robbie joined in, despite his embarrassment. The truth was that Mr. Rumsey was one of the most popular teachers in the school, one who could make even the densest math theorems sound interesting.

Well, *almost* interesting.

"It's not you, Mr. R.," Robbie said, when the class had settled down. "I was just, um . . . thinking about something."

"Ah, yes, and I believe I know what it is," Mr. Rumsey said. "I heard there was some excitement this weekend. At the carnival, wasn't it? Something about a young man performing some sort of athletic feat that had to be seen to be believed."

The rest of the class was smiling and looking at Robbie. His face felt even hotter.

And he thought: Even the teachers know?

"Yes, well, I can see how that could consume one's thoughts," Mr. R. continued. "But if you'd be good enough to put aside thoughts of your amazing evening and focus on the lesson plan at hand, calculating perimeter and circumference—oh, the excitement; be still my heart!—we'll get on with it."

Robbie nodded vigorously, eager to get everyone's eyes off him. This was getting ridiculous. Even his mom and dad had talked nonstop about his throws at the carnival over the weekend. What's next, he thought, a big story in the local newspaper? A TV crew camped on his front lawn, waiting for an exclusive interview?

It just wasn't that big of a deal. Heck, even as a little kid, he had always had a great aim.

Well, at least BSA.

Before Stevie Altman.

Ninety minutes later, Robbie was eating lunch in the cafeteria. Marty was off somewhere completing a science project, so Robbie sat alone in the back, holding a textbook in front of his face, trying to look inconspicuous.

But he quickly found himself thinking, This is a pretty dumb thing to do if you don't want to be noticed. What kid reads a textbook at lunch? Not even the biggest nerds in the school did that.

Marty wouldn't even do it!

Suddenly, three brown paper bags plopped on the table, almost in unison. Robbie looked up. Smiling down at him were Jordy, Connor, and Willie.

"These seats taken?" Jordy asked.

Robbie's eyes widened. He tried to come up with a funny, smart-alecky reply, but his mind went blank. Jordy, Connor, and Willie always sat up front, with all the cool kids. What were they doing back here in Loserville?

"No, they're all yours," Robbie said finally, thinking: Oh, that's a snappy comeback. Way to think on your feet.

"Excellent," Willie said as the three sat down. He held out his fist for a bump. "We good? Or are you still mad at me?"

Robbie returned the bump and said, "We're good."

Willie nodded, still smiling. The three boys rustled through their bags and pulled out sandwiches, chips, and water bottles.

"That was incredible, dude," Jordy said finally. "The other night? At the carnival?"

Robbie shrugged. "I got lucky," he replied. "Like Willie said."

All three boys shook their heads.

"No way," Connor said. "Nine times in a row isn't luck. And you made it look so easy!"

"Throwing some heat, too!" Willie said. "Didn't even look like you aimed!"

He clambered to his feet suddenly and imitated Robbie's smooth, graceful windup, pretending to uncork a blazing fastball at an unseen hitter without even looking. The kids at the next table stared. The cafeteria monitor, a nervous teacher named Mrs. Niedermeyer, peered at him over her reading glasses, ever alert for trouble. Was mass rebellion in the air?

"So we want to know something," Willie said, sitting back down. He looked expectantly at Connor.

"Oh, um, right," Connor said. "We want to know why— seeing as how, y'know, you could do what you did at the carnival—how come you don't—?"

"How come I don't throw like that in games?" Robbie said, nodding. "How come I'm all over the place? How come I walk so many batters? How come I basically—let's just come out and say it—suck at pitching for the Orioles?"

The three boys looked uneasily at each other, then back at Robbie.

"That's what you want to know, right?" he asked.

They nodded sheepishly.

Robbie put down his sandwich. There was a faraway look in his eyes now.

"Ever see a pitcher hit a kid so hard the ball slams off the kid's batting helmet and goes all the way back to the mound—on the fly?" he said. "So hard the helmet actually cracks in half? And paint from the helmet is on the ball?"

The three boys stared at Robbie. For several seconds, no one spoke.

Finally, Willie snorted dismissively. "Yeah, right," he said. "Like that's ever happened."

Connor laughed, too. "That's crazy!" he said. "What kid throws that hard? No kid around here."

But Jordy kept staring at Robbie, a question forming on

his lips. "Are you saying that actually happened?" he asked finally.

Robbie took a deep breath and thought: Okay, this is it. Time to tell them. Hope they don't think I'm a big baby. Or laugh at me for being such a wuss.

He felt strangely calm, though. After all these months, maybe it would be good to get it all out.

Just then, Mrs. Niedermeyer clapped her hands briskly and announced, "People, we're having problems with the bell today! Lunch is over! Please move on to your next class!"

Now the cafeteria erupted with the sounds of lunch bags being tossed in the trash, trays clattering, and students chatting loudly as they headed for the doors.

Jordy was still staring at Robbie when they reached the hallway.

But all Robbie said was, "See you at practice, okay?" Then he turned and walked away.

He felt like a woozy boxer who had come *this* close to making a big mistake in the ring.

Saved by the bell.

Again.

Well, sort of.

The Orioles were gathered around the backstop of a dusty field across town, waiting for Ray Hammond to finish raking the batter's box and tying down the bases. It was a hot, humid afternoon, and from beyond the thick stand of trees on the other side of the park they could hear the happy sounds of kids laughing and splashing. Through the branches they caught an occasional glimpse of shimmering blue water and a bone-white diving board.

"Ah, a unique form of torture," Marty had said when they first arrived. "Holding a practice in ninety-five-degree heat next to a community pool."

At the moment, though, the topic of conversation among the Orioles was: how much do we stink?

And the consensus opinion seemed to be: we stink a whole lot.

"Now other teams are calling us the Snore-ioles," Jordy said, listlessly fanning himself with his cap.

"Or instead of the O's, they call us the No's," Connor said.

"Or the Zeros," Joey said. "Heard that one in school today."

Willie banged the handle of his bat in the sun-baked dirt and spat out a mouthful of sunflower seeds.

"Guys, we're oh-and-nine!" he said. "Oh-and-freaking-nine! What do you expect them to call us? The Orioles: a legendary baseball powerhouse?"

"Anything but the Zeros," Joey said, shaking his head. "I'm sorry. That's just . . . *wrong*."

For a moment, no one spoke. A warm breeze rustled through the trees. The sounds wafting from the pool seemed even louder now.

"Here's a question," Mike said finally. "Has any team in this league ever gone a whole season without a win?"

"If anyone can do it," Jordy said morosely, "we can."

"There's the fighting spirit, Jordy," Willie said, shooting him a look. "There's the old never-say-die attitude."

"Wow," Connor said. "Think about it! No wins for an entire season! That would majorly suck."

"Maybe," Marty said. "But maybe not. No, hear me out for a sec."

He sauntered to the front of the group and held up his hands for attention. "Okay, imagine for a second that we're the worst team ever," he said. "Not just in the league, I mean in the whole history of organized baseball! We're so bad we're on *SportsCenter*. ESPN does a docudrama about us—that's part documentary, part drama for you slow guys like Joey over there. Then, of course, someone makes a movie about us. And we all get to play ourselves in the movie! And suddenly we're celebrities!"

He had a faraway look in his eyes now.

"From that point on, wherever we go, people say,

'Look, it's the Orioles, the world-famous losers! We want to party with you, dudes!' Suddenly fans are hitting us up for autographs, buying us free meals, introducing us to hot chicks—just so they can hang out with us!"

He spread his arms wide, looked excitedly at his team-mates, and said, "Wouldn't that be *so cool*?"

Everyone stared at him in disbelief.

"Okay, fine," Marty murmured, plopping down on the grass. "It was just a thought."

"A really *dumb* thought," Willie said.

"Really, really dumb," Joey said. "Dumb to, like, the two hundredth power."

"Whatever," Marty said. "But 'bad' sells. I just watched a YouTube video of the worst dancer in the world. The guy gets ten thousand hits a month. He's a big star now. I rest my case."

Watching his buddy pout, Robbie found himself grinning. During the entire discussion, Robbie had kept reminding himself to keep his mouth shut. Now that the Orioles were being friendly to him again, still dazzled by his exploits at the carnival a few days ago, he didn't want to say something stupid to tick them off.

Also, Robbie knew that part of the reason the Orioles were winless—no, the *major* reason they were winless—was because of his crappy pitching. No sense calling attention to that inconvenient fact, in case one of the Orioles were to stand up, point a finger at him, and scream, "YOU! YOU'RE WHY WE SUCK!"

Just then Ray Hammond called them together. He put down his rake and wiped his brow. "All right, it's hot as blazes," he said. "We'll hit and call it a day. I'll pitch. Willie, Jordy, and Connor, you're up first. Everyone else shags balls."

As the Orioles turned to go, Coach grinned. "Oh, one more thing," he said. "I'm calling home-run derby. Everyone gets fifteen swings. Winner gets a giant snowball at the Snack Shack. My treat."

The Orioles let out a cheer and ran off to get started. Soon they were having so much fun swinging out of their shoes they forgot about the oppressive heat. Connor was the early home-run king with four jacks, until Carlos topped him with five bombs, including a mammoth shot over the fence in dead-center field.

"I'll probably regret this," Coach said at one point. "Probably mess up your swings. But we have to live a little, right?"

Finally, Joey stepped into the batter's box, the last hitter of the afternoon. Not far away, in a shady patch of grass behind first base, a dad sat next to a stroller with a toddler strapped into it. Every once in a while he pointed toward the Orioles and whispered to the child, as if giving him his first baseball lesson.

Wow, Robbie thought. How bored do you have to be to watch us practice? Be careful, mister. Watching the Zeros play might traumatize that kid for life.

Seconds later, something amazing happened.

On his very first swing, Joey ripped a vicious foul ball down the first base line. It was headed straight for the stroller. The Orioles gasped as one.

Suddenly there was a flash of movement in the shadows

and a hand reached out and speared the ball. The hand belonged to a tall boy with long, floppy blond hair who appeared to be about thirteen.

The boy grinned and pointed at the startled father, as if to say, *You owe me one, buddy. Saved your kid's butt.* Then he flipped the ball nonchalantly behind his back to Jordy, like what he'd just done was the easiest thing in the whole world.

But that wasn't the most amazing thing.

The most amazing thing was this: the boy had only one arm.

"Did . . . you . . . see . . . that?" Willie said, wide-eyed with astonishment.

Robbie nodded uncertainly, still staring at the boy. "I . . . *think* so," he said. "It was like something out of a movie."

The boy wore a white T-shirt, baggy plaid shorts, and flip-flops. For the rest of Joey's swings, he stood in the shade near the stroller, watching the Orioles intently.

As soon as practice was over, Robbie jogged over to him. Which was when the boy took off, running hard in his flip-flops, going faster than Robbie had ever seen a kid go.

"Hey, wait up!" Robbie yelled.

The boy looked back. For an instant, he seemed to smile. But he didn't stop.

He ran past the Snack Shack, through the parking lot, and into the trees.

Then he was gone.

There was a note on the kitchen counter when Robbie, Ashley, and their dad arrived home that evening. Robbie and his dad were exhausted from practice. Ashley, on the other hand, seemed hyper after spending the afternoon at her friend's house.

The note read:

Reminder: Big gig tonight for Catering by Mary. You're on your own for dinner. I know this is an awesome responsibility. Don't blow it!
Love,
Mom

"No problem," Ray Hammond said, reaching for the phone. "This is why they invented pizza. Pepperoni or sausage?"

"Pepperoni, sausage, *and* extra cheese," Robbie said.

"Ewww!" Ashley said. "Gross!" Then she smiled. "Actually, it doesn't sound bad."

Their dad grinned. "The Heart Attack Special," he said.

"Good choice. I can feel my arteries clogging already."

Robbie couldn't stop thinking about the one-armed boy. The kid had been a blur racing to make the catch. And what hand-eye coordination! Then there was the cool behind-the-back toss to Jordy—now *there* was some serious swagger! It was like the cherry on top of an ice cream sundae. Plus the kid had seemed so confident—something Robbie definitely wasn't right now.

He wondered what had happened to the kid's arm. Car accident? Power tool mishap? Or some horrible disease that had required amputation to save his life?

And why had the boy run away when Robbie approached him? He certainly didn't seem ashamed of having one arm. No, there was nothing in his bearing that suggested the kid was anything but self-assured, to the point of being cocky.

Was the kid not supposed to be at the field that day? Or did he suddenly realize he was due somewhere else when Robbie trotted over to talk to him?

The more Robbie thought about the kid, the more questions leaped to his mind.

Did the kid have a family? Did he go to school in the area? Did he play baseball? Robbie knew there were kids with disabilities who did all sorts of amazing things in sports. Just the other day he'd watched a video of a one-armed boy in California with a blazing fastball and killer curve who was the best pitcher in his league and the talk of the whole community.

This kid who had dazzled the Orioles yesterday—he was an athlete too. Robbie was sure of it. Everything about the kid said he was a baller—or had been at some point in his life. You didn't move like that, didn't make a catch like that, if you'd never played the game.

It would be like me strapping on skates, dashing the length of the rink with the puck, and scoring on some ridiculous slap shot when I've never played hockey in my life, Robbie thought. Uh-uh. This kid knew baseball. Just the way he handled the ball told you that.

And what about that mysterious smile the kid had flashed as he ran away? What was that all about? Was that his way of saying, *Ha, ha, forget it, kid. You don't have a prayer of catching me*?

No, Robbie didn't think so. He couldn't swear to it, but there almost seemed to be something sad about that smile. Almost like the kid was saying, *Sorry, but I can't talk right now*.

The pizza arrived thirty minutes later, delivered by a heavyset man who was wheezing after climbing the five steps to the front door.

"Now there's a guy who should probably cut back on his own product," Ray Hammond said after the man left. Laughing, Robbie and Ashley agreed.

They ate on the back deck. It was cooler now; the sun was beginning to set, and a soft breeze rippled through the garden as they hungrily attacked their meal.

"That boy at practice today . . ." Robbie said after a few minutes.

"What boy?" Ashley said suspiciously.

Quickly, Robbie filled her in on the one-armed boy's appearance.

"Still thinking about him, huh?" their dad said. "I can

see why. Pretty impressive catch. Even for someone with both arms."

Robbie nodded. "He's a hero, too. He might have saved that little kid's life."

"You're always so dramatic," Ashley said, rolling her eyes.

"No, Robbie could be right," their dad said. "The ball was sure tracking that way."

"I wonder what it's like," Robbie said. "Having only one arm . . . ?"

His dad reached for another slice and shook his head. "Can't be easy," he said. "But people have overcome disabilities since the beginning of time. A guy with one arm even played in the major leagues."

"How can a one-armed person play baseball?" Ashley said. "That doesn't make sense."

"Well, it happened," Ray Hammond said. "Pete Gray. An outfielder. Played for the old St. Louis Browns during World War Two. Google it if you don't believe me."

"Oh, I intend to," Ashley said, taking a bite of her pizza.

"What happened to his arm?" Robbie asked.

"He fell off a farmer's wagon when he was a little kid," his dad said. "Got caught in the wagon's spokes. His arm had to be amputated above the elbow."

Robbie and Ashley winced. Robbie tried to imagine how terrifying that must have been for little Pete Gray, or Petey, or whatever they called him. One minute you're a perfectly healthy kid, the next minute they're wheeling you into a hospital, knocking you out, and sawing off your arm.

If they even had hospitals back then.

And anesthesia.

Robbie shuddered just thinking about it.

"Then there was a guy who pitched in the majors with only one hand," Ray Hammond said.

"Okay, that did it!" Ashley said. "Now you're just telling stories."

"Nope. His name was Jim Abbott. Pitched for a bunch of teams—Angels, Yankees, Red Sox, maybe a couple more. This was in the 1980s and 1990s. You should've seen this guy. Unbelievable."

"But what if they hit it back to him?" Robbie asked. "How did he—?"

"He was a lefty," his dad said. "Kept the glove on the end of his right arm. Soon as he pitched, he slipped the glove on his left hand to field the ball. Then he'd hold the glove against his body, grab the ball, and throw the runner out. He was so smooth doing it, too."

Robbie and Ashley stared disbelievingly at their dad.

"Bet if you go on YouTube, you'll find video of him pitching," Ray Hammond said. "He was an inspiration to a lot of folks."

"I gotta see that!" Ashley said, jumping from her seat. "Okay if I use the computer now? I'm all finished. How can you two eat so much? That's so gross!"

Robbie and his dad smiled at each other as she went inside. They could hear her bounding down the stairs to the family room.

"Here's one more one-armed story for you," his dad said. "Not a ballplayer, though. The drummer for the band Def Leppard."

"A one-armed drummer?" Robbie said.

"He had a special drum set custom-made for him. And he taught himself to play. I saw him in concert once. He was great."

The sun was low on the horizon and crickets were beginning to chirp. Ray Hammond glanced at the pizza box and sighed with contentment. Only one small slice remained, along with four or five forlorn crusts that looked as if they had been gnawed on by tiny woodland creatures.

"I'm stuffed," his dad said. "I don't think I can move. You might have to roll me inside."

"As long as I don't have to throw you," Robbie said, grinning. "You know how that would go. Low and outside."

Ray Hammond shook his head. "Not for much longer," he said. "I got a feeling the old Robbie Hammond is about to make a comeback."

"That would be nice," Robbie said as they both stood. "Now all I want to know is when."

"Hopefully soon," his dad said. "Because you're pitching Friday. Against the Yankees."

Robbie looked at his dad and gulped hard.

He felt a strange gurgling in his stomach now.

And it wasn't from the pizza.

The Orioles had just begun their warm-ups when a caravan of gleaming SUVs snaked up the long winding road next to Eddie Murray Field and pulled into the parking lot. Out spilled a dozen boys wearing immaculate pinstriped uniforms and navy-blue caps, laughing and high-fiving each other as their coaches and parents hurried along behind with the equipment.

It could only mean one thing: the Yankees were in the house.

The first-place, undefeated Yankees.

"Un-freaking-believable," Jordy said as the Yankees paraded past, headed to their dugout.

The Orioles had never seen anything like it.

Not only were the Yankees wearing the brightest uniforms anyone had ever seen, they also wore matching warm-up jackets and matching spikes and carried matching gear bags.

It got worse. They were also wearing matching white puka-shell necklaces, which the Orioles discovered when the Yankees pulled off their jackets.

Willie couldn't resist. "Aren't we accessorized today!" he shouted. "Who are you guys, the Barbie Doll Yankees?"

As the Orioles cracked up, a few of the Yankees looked over and glared. Another, a tall boy with red hair and thick shoulders, stepped toward Willie.

"You're about to find out who we are, shorty," the kid said.

"Oooooh!" the Orioles said in unison.

"Yo, easy, Red!" Willie said. "It's just that you're all looking so sharp! Matching boxers, too?"

Now the other boy's face turned as red as his hair. "You need to shut it. I don't know why you think you can even talk to us. When was the last time you guys won a game?" he shouted. "Oh, that's right. That would be *never*, wouldn't it?"

"Okay," Willie said, shrugging and turning back to the Orioles. "I got nothing for that one."

Neither did anyone else. The redheaded kid smiled triumphantly and went back to his team.

By game time the Yankees' parents had set up camp down the right field line, where they sat under Yankees sun umbrellas and Yankees tents while fishing water bottles and soda cans from Yankees coolers.

They had even set up a Yankees misting station where the players could go to cool off, even though it was a cloudy day and not overly warm.

"*A misting station!*" Jordy said, staring out at the scene in wonder.

"Bet it has a flat-screen TV, too," Connor said.

"And probably a Jacuzzi," Mike said.

When the Yankees took the field to start the game, the

Orioles made yet another discovery, this one more than a little unsettling: the big redhead was on the mound.

And throwing hard.

"Mad hard," Willie said, watching from the on-deck circle as the kid warmed up. "Naturally, the biggest, meanest kid on the other team, the one I tick off with my big mouth, turns out to be their flame-throwing all-star pitcher. It never fails."

"Yeah, thanks a lot, Willie," Joey said as the rest of the Orioles nodded somberly.

"Big deal!" a voice cried.

It was Marty. He leaped off the bench, walked to the middle of the dugout, and pointed at Robbie.

"So what if they have Big Red?" Marty said. "We got our own flame-throwing intimidator, and his name is Robert W. Hammond. My man right here."

"Your middle name is *W*?" Joey said, looking at Robbie. "That's it? Just an initial?"

Marty shook his head wearily and massaged his temple with both thumbs, as if fending off a massive headache.

"The *W* stands for William, you idiot!" he said as the rest of the Orioles chuckled. "And you witnessed his skill the other night at the carnival. No, my man is going to be the best pitcher this league has ever seen. Once he gets past some, uh, minor control issues. . . ."

"Marty," Robbie said, "why don't we just—"

"Please, Robbie," Marty said, holding up a hand. "Let me handle this."

He turned back to the Orioles, who were grinning now, amused by the performance.

"And that's not all," Marty continued. "My man is going out there today, and he will match Big Red pitch for pitch. He'll whistle fastballs past the Yankees, snap off curves, and drop changeups that'll have them drilling themselves into the batter's box!"

"Marty . . ." Robbie said, but again there was the hand.

"So we are not going to worry about big, fat, ugly Red over there!" Marty thundered. "Because, gentlemen, Robert William Hammond has our backs. He will not fail us. The legend begins today."

With that he plopped down next to Robbie, smacked him on the thigh, and said loudly, "Now go get 'em, big guy."

Robbie glared at him. "Are you out of your mind?!" he hissed. "Could you *possibly* put more pressure on me?"

But Marty just smiled serenely. It was, Robbie realized, typical Marty. Sometimes you didn't know whether to hug him or choke him.

Predictably, Big Red's stuff was nasty.

Willie barely got around on a low fastball and grounded out meekly to first base. Joey struck out on four pitches. Jordy tried to work the count and slow down the big right-hander's momentum by stepping out after every pitch. But eventually he went down on a 3–2 fastball that just caught the outside of the plate.

Three up, three down for the O's. Just like that.

As he strutted off the mound at the end of the inning, Big Red turned to the Orioles dugout and snarled, "Yo, Snore-ioles! I'll be bringing it like that all game!"

This time, no one said anything back. Marty tried, but Willie lunged and clamped a hand over his mouth.

"Shhh, this guy's too good," Willie whispered as Marty, bug-eyed, struggled to speak. "Don't get him any more riled up!"

As he warmed up with Joey, Robbie was pleasantly surprised to find his pitches actually going where he wanted them to—well, most of the time. And it carried over to the real game.

The Yankees leadoff hitter popped out to Jordy at first. Robbie fell behind 3–0 to the next batter, but then grooved two strikes before the kid swung at an outside pitch and bounced out to Willie. And the next kid swung at a pitch headed for the dirt and hit a comebacker to the mound, which Robbie fielded easily for the third out.

Robbie knew he wasn't throwing nearly as hard as he had in the old pre-Stevie days. But at least he was around the plate today, which felt like a major accomplishment. For the first time in weeks, he left the mound with a bounce in his step.

As the rest of the Orioles clapped him on the back and said, "Good job," Marty made a beeline in from right field.

"Whoa, what happened *there*?" Marty said. "A psychological breakthrough? Has the Terrible Curse of Wildness been lifted?"

"Not sure," Robbie said. "But how 'bout we do this? How 'bout we see if I can do it again next inning before you start yapping about that legend stuff?"

"Understood," Marty said, pretending to zip his mouth. "Not another word. Don't want to ruin the karma."

"Yeah," Robbie said, grinning. "Whatever you want to call it, don't ruin it."

It was another one-two-three inning for the Orioles at the plate, and Robbie felt like he was back on the mound in no time.

The Yankees cleanup hitter was due up. Curious to see who it was, Robbie looked over at their dugout. A massive head covered with a shiny blue helmet emerged first, followed by a pair of enormous shoulders and then the rest of the torso.

It was Big Red.

He sauntered to the on-deck circle, carrying a huge black bat, the biggest Robbie had ever seen. Staring at Robbie the whole time, he took three vicious cuts, swinging so hard the bat seemed to whistle as it cut through the air.

After Robbie's last warm-up toss, Joey shuffled to the mound and pulled off his mask. "Just a suggestion," he said. "But I would pitch this guy carefully. *Very* carefully."

"Ya think?" Robbie said. He looked nervously at Big Red again. "Did he have those muscles when the game started?"

"I think they're new," Joey said. "Thought I saw him bench-pressing your dad's car between innings."

As Big Red dug in at the plate, Robbie took a deep breath. A thought occurred to him: Maybe the kid's dumb. Maybe he'll swing at junk.

His first pitch was low and outside. His second pitch was high and outside. But Big Red wasn't chasing. With a smirk, he stepped out and took another vicious swing, eyes still locked on Robbie.

Okay, Robbie thought, what do I do now? He knew what his dad would say. *You go right after the hitter. You challenge him. You don't back down.* Even with the semi-crappy fastball he'd been throwing? *Yeah, even with that.*

Robbie peered in for the sign from Joey. Fastball. He wound up, kicked high, and fired. Decent pitch, he thought, as the ball left his hand. Except now it was headed directly over the plate and Big Red's eyes were lighting up and Robbie was already cringing.

Big Red swung. There was a flash of black and then the muffled sound of metal meeting horsehide—*pingggg*!

Robbie whipped around in time to see the ball soaring over the left field fence until it was just a tiny dot in the sky.

He wondered if it would ever come down.

And if so, where.

Maybe someplace in Montana, he decided.

Big Red flipped the bat and stood at the plate, watching the mammoth blast leave the ball field. Only then did he break into his home run trot, grinning at each of the slack-jawed Orioles infielders as he went by. It was the slowest home run trot any of them had ever seen, possibly the slowest in league history.

"Look at that big jerk!" said Joey, walking out to the mound again. "Who does he think he is? Big Papi Ortiz? Prince Freaking Fielder?"

But Robbie didn't much care how long it took Big Red to circle the bases. When you hit 'em that far, you deserve to celebrate, he thought. That's what I get for throwing that slow slop up there. And leaving it out over the plate.

The realization made him wistful. He wished he could have faced Big Red with his old fastball, the one that had batters swinging at air all last season. The one that dazzled everyone at the Brooks Robinson Camp, including all those hoary coaches.

Big Red was obviously big and strong, and a good

hitter. But could he have caught up to Robbie's old heater? Could he have turned on a seventy-mile-per-hour Robbie Hammond lightning bolt up around his eyes?

"Guess we'll never know," he murmured to himself.

When Big Red finally crossed the plate, he looked back at Robbie and sneered.

"That's the best you got?" he yelled. "Because that was *weak!* My grandma throws faster than that."

"Play ball, son," the umpire barked. "Save the trash talk for someplace else."

"Sure, ump," Big Red said, flashing a sarcastic smile. "Whatever you say."

"Really?" the umpire said, ripping off his mask. He was steaming. "In that case, I say this: one more word out of you and you're gone."

The big kid snapped off a yes-sir salute and swaggered off, the ump staring at him until he disappeared in the dugout.

Robbie was rattled by the home run. His wildness promptly returned and he walked the next two batters. The runners tagged and moved up on a fly ball to Yancy in center field. Robbie got the next batter on a bouncer back to the mound for the second out. But the next batter smacked another of Robbie's "grandma fastballs" up the middle for a two-run single.

Now Robbie was seething at himself for letting the Yankees number nine hitter beat him. He pounded the ball in his glove and gritted his teeth as he looked in at the next batter. Throwing harder, he ran the count to 2 and 2 before the kid swung at a low fastball for strike three.

But the damage was done.

Yankees 3, Orioles 0.

This time Robbie walked off the mound with his head down.

"Okay, not bad, not bad!" his dad said, clapping. "Saw some encouraging signs! You're getting there!"

Robbie was in no mood to listen to any of that. He slammed his glove against the dugout wall and took a seat at the end of the bench, his shoulders slumped.

When Marty sat down next to him, Robbie shot him a look.

"What?" Marty said. "Is this a bad time?"

"If you ever mention that legend stuff again," Robbie said quietly, "I might have to kill you."

Marty's eyes widened. But for once, he said nothing.

Big Red was still breezing through the Orioles' batting order in the top of the third inning. He was grunting— *Uhhh!*—after every pitch now. And the grunting was getting louder and louder, as if the kid was determined to show everyone how hard he was working.

"I *hate* grunters," Willie said, looking out at Big Red. "He's just showing off."

"Why don't you go tell him that?" Jordy said.

"Yeah," Connor said. "Put him in an even better mood."

That inning, Yancy had the first decent at-bat against the big kid, but his sharp line drive screamed right at the Yankees left fielder for the first out. Riley struck out on four pitches. Robbie was up next.

Seeing Robbie dig in, Big Red smirked again and started to say something. But the umpire stepped quickly from behind the plate, pointed a finger at him, and said simply, "Don't."

Robbie took the first two pitches, both low, seeing what the big guy had. Big Red threw hard, sure, but he wasn't the fastest kid Robbie had ever faced. And his fastball didn't move as much as Robbie expected it to, either.

I can hit this guy, he thought. Unless I'm just fooling myself. Unless I'm doing the baseball equivalent of whistling past the graveyard.

He took a called strike, then watched as Big Red's next pitch sailed outside. On the next pitch, he was late swinging at a belt-high fastball, fouling it off to the right.

The count was 3 and 2. Robbie stepped out and took a deep breath. Don't give in, don't give in, he kept telling himself. And he didn't. Instead, he fouled off the next pitch. And the next one. And the one after that, too.

"Way to hang!" his dad yelled. The rest of the Orioles were whooping, too, enthralled with the mini-drama that had suddenly developed between the big kid and their pitcher. There was also the sheer joy of seeing Big Red getting more and more frustrated, grunting louder and louder, his face turning redder and redder with each pitch.

Still, Robbie didn't give in.

He fouled off another pitch, then another, then two more. Stomping around the mound after each pitch, Big Red looked like he wanted to scream. Instead, he bit down on his glove, setting off a gale of laughter in the Orioles dugout.

Please, guys, Robbie thought. The kid's head is about to explode as it is. Don't make it worse.

Finally, on the thirteenth pitch of the at-bat, Robbie hit a sharp one-hopper up the middle that the shortstop gloved on a nice play, firing on to first to end the inning.

Big Red pumped his fist and yelled like he had just struck out Alex Rodriguez with the bases loaded in the World Series. Still, Robbie was proud of himself. At least he'd hung in there and made the big guy work, big-time. At least he hadn't swung at any junk. In some ways, it had been his best at-bat of the year.

When Mike relieved him in the fourth inning, the Orioles were still down, 3–0. But Robbie had to grudgingly admit it had been his best pitching outing of the season, too. Sure, the velocity hadn't been there—his fastball wasn't even close to what it used to be. But at least he had only walked two guys. He'd managed to keep his team in the game.

As the afternoon went on, he found his gloom lifting, especially when the Orioles staged a mini-rally in the sixth inning off the Yankees relief pitcher. Willie drew a leadoff walk, Jordy moved him over with a bouncer to first, and Connor delivered a run-scoring double to pull the Orioles to 3–1.

But that was how it ended: 3–1 Yankees, with Yancy making the final out on a long fly ball to center field. It was the Orioles' tenth loss in a row. Yet somehow this one hurt less than the others, maybe because they knew they had just given a good team all it could handle.

After the two teams lined up to slap hands, Big Red went down the line slapping extra hard and muttering, "You suck, you suck" under his breath instead of "Good game, good game."

When he reached Robbie, he stopped and smiled coldly. "Your coach got you out of there just in time," he said. "My next at-bat might have torn your head off."

"Oh, yeah?" Marty said, whirling around and getting in Big Red's face. He jabbed a finger in Robbie's direction. "Next time he faces you, you'll be lucky if you *see* the ball."

It was really kind of comical, Robbie thought, seeing that the top of Marty's head barely came up to Big Red's throat.

"Who's this?" the big kid asked Robbie. "Your nerd bodyguard?"

Robbie started to answer. Just then, he caught a glimpse of something over Big Red's shoulder. The sight made him freeze.

There was the one-armed boy, leaning against the fence, watching them intently. Only, this time he was wearing a hat.

The hat was on backward, but the orange band and black trim were a dead giveaway.

It was an Orioles hat.

"Uh, love to stay and chat," Robbie said. "But I gotta go."

He tossed his glove nonchalantly toward the dugout. Then he took off on a dead run for the one-armed boy.

This time, Robbie thought, he's not getting away.

The boy bolted again. Seeing Robbie coming, he turned and sprinted for the parking lot, long legs churning, blue flip-flops slapping rhythmically against the asphalt.

"Dad, see you at home!" Robbie yelled over his shoulder.

Even with his stubby SpongeBob build, Robbie considered himself a pretty fast runner. But it soon became obvious he couldn't catch the one-armed boy—at least not without a rocket pack strapped to his back.

If I can just keep him in sight, Robbie thought, maybe I'll find out where he lives. Or maybe he'll get tired and stop running.

Robbie chased the boy down the long, winding road that led to Eddie Murray Field, then down another road and up a hill. Most of the time the boy was a good two hundred yards ahead, looking back occasionally to see if Robbie was still there. As they neared the top of the hill, Robbie started to catch up. The kid was definitely tiring now. Which was a good thing, since Robbie's lungs were burning and his side was beginning to cramp.

Still, it wasn't until they had run another quarter mile,

past office buildings and an empty field, that the boy finally staggered to a stop.

"Okay . . . you . . . got . . . me!" he said, gasping for breath. "What do you want?"

Robbie was so exhausted he wasn't sure. He was bent over at the waist, hands on his knees, chest heaving.

"I . . . guess I just want to talk," he said.

The boy nodded, as if that was the answer he expected. "Okay, go ahead. Talk."

"What's your name?" Robbie asked.

"They call me Lefty." The boy gazed at the dangling sleeve of his T-shirt, where his right arm should have been. Seeing the horrified look on Robbie's face, he said, "Relax! I'm kidding! It's Ben. Ben Landrum."

He threw himself down on a patch of grass and wiped the sweat from his brow. "Go ahead," he said. "Ask me."

Robbie looked at him quizzically.

"Ask what happened to my arm!" the boy said, looking annoyed. "That's what you want to know, isn't it?"

"Okay," Robbie said. "What happened to your arm?"

"Shark chewed it off. Swallowed the whole thing. In one giant bite."

Robbie's jaw dropped.

"Nah, just messing with you," Ben said. "The real story's kind of boring. So I come up with what my therapist calls 'alternative narrations' that are more exciting. Told one kid I lost the arm in a sword fight." He laughed mirthlessly. "Jerk actually believed it, too."

Ben watched a few cars go by and seemed lost in thought. "Thing is," he continued, "I've told so many different stories

I can't keep track of them all. I forget which story I've told to which person."

"I want the *real* story," Robbie said. He waved at the big hill they had just run up. "You owe it to me. Look how far you made me run."

Ben managed a weak grin. "Okay," he said. "You want to hear the whole thing? Or the CliffsNotes version?"

"I'm in no hurry," Robbie said, plopping down beside him.

Ben shrugged. "Like I said, it's not very exciting," he said. "I had a dirt bike. Bought it off a friend who'd stopped riding. My mom didn't want me to get it—she said it was too dangerous. But I didn't listen. I had this money my grandma gave me. And I cried and whined and pleaded until my mom said, 'Fine, go get the stupid bike!' Just to shut me up."

Robbie nodded. Been there, done that with the whining and pleading to parents, he thought.

"At first I just rode near my house," Ben continued. "My mom wouldn't let me ride anywhere else. But she's always at work, so pretty soon I started riding wherever I wanted.

"Then these older kids told me about some trails deep in the woods. I never should've gone with them. But I did, one day right after school. The trails were crazy steep and winding. The other kids were all better riders than me, way more experienced. I never should've . . ."

He took a deep breath and said, "Okay, now we're getting to the good part—if you want to call it that. It happened on our first run. I was going too fast. I hit a bump and flew way up in the air. The bike came down on my arm.

The metal practically tore through the whole thing. Two of the kids freaked out and just ran off. One went for help. But we were deep in the woods. It took a long time for the paramedics to get there. Forever, it seemed."

Robbie shuddered at the thought of Ben being in such horrible pain for so long.

"I woke up in the hospital, and my mom was leaning over the bed, crying. There were two doctors in the room. She told me my arm had been cut real bad. A lot of nerves and tendons were severed. She said they were taking me into surgery and there was a chance the arm would have to be amputated."

He stared at the empty sleeve of his T-shirt again. "When I woke up, it was gone. That's it. End of story. Pretty boring, huh?"

Ben seemed to be studying him now, waiting for his reaction. But Robbie didn't know what to say. He looked away for a moment, trying to gather his thoughts.

"When did it happen?" he asked finally.

"Let's see . . . sixteen months, fourteen days, and—what time is it, around five o'clock?—two hours ago," Ben said. "Not that I've been keeping track."

A cool breeze was rippling through the field now, and he closed his eyes and held his face to the sun. "Know what the hardest part is?" he said. "It's not what you might think. It's not tying your shoes, or buttoning your shirt, or cutting a steak. It's . . . being *different*. Having people stare at you all the time. Hearing the same questions. It makes you crazy."

He shook his head. "That's why I ran. I knew what you wanted."

"No, it's not about that," Robbie said. "It's just . . . you made that great catch. At our practice."

Ben nodded and smiled. "Liked that one, huh? Yeah, the one-armed dude came through. That little kid in the stroller, he might've had *Rawlings* tattooed on his forehead."

Robbie nodded. "But why were you even watching us? We're, like, the worst team that's ever played."

"I was going to the pool," Ben said. "You want to see people stare? Try being a one-armed kid and going swimming. But then I saw you guys practicing. Baseball is my all-time favorite sport. Played it for years until . . ." He lifted his right shoulder. "*This.*"

A wistful look crossed his face. "Then I found out your games are at that field down the road," he continued, "so I came over today to watch."

"Your missing arm," Robbie said. "No offense, but were you a righty or—?"

"No, I was a lefty before the accident," he said. "That was about the only good luck I had. Didn't have to learn to write and throw all over again."

In his mind, Robbie replayed the terrific catch Ben had made the other day: the quick, loping strides to get to the ball, the ease with which he had hauled it in, the fancy flip to Jordy at the end.

How many other kids could make a play like that?

"You'll play ball again!" Robbie blurted, more forcefully than he'd intended. "I *know* you will!"

Ben smiled wearily. "That's what my mom says, too."

"We have another practice Thursday," Robbie said. "Four o'clock. Same field as the other day. You should come."

Ben stared at him for a moment, then climbed to his feet. "I have to go," he said. Without another word, he turned and began running back down the hill.

"Hey!" Robbie yelled. "Where do you live? Where do you go to school?"

The one-armed boy waved, but he didn't stop.

Soon he went around a bend and disappeared.

Marty wrinkled his nose and swung the tip of his fishing rod over to Robbie. A small bluegill wriggled and danced on the end of the line.

"Okay, take it off," Marty said, suddenly looking pale.

Robbie gaped at him. "Let me get this straight," he said. "*You* just caught a fish. But you want *me* to unhook it?"

"I don't touch fish," Marty said.

"You're fishing and you don't touch fish?"

"Correct," Marty said. "It's a long-standing policy of mine. Dates back many years."

"That's like saying, 'I'm going bowling, but I won't touch the bowling ball,'" Robbie said.

"No, it's not," Marty said. "Bowling balls can't bite. Bowling balls can't attack you and tear your flesh and leave blood spurting everywhere."

Robbie considered the tiny fish, glinting in the bright sunshine. "Marty," he said, "it's a six-inch bluegill, not a barracuda."

"Still," Marty said, "I don't touch fish. No exceptions.

I don't touch frogs or turtles, either. And definitely not snakes." He shuddered.

"Is that why we had to use cut-up hot dogs for bait?" Robbie asked. "Instead of worms?"

"Precisely. Now you're catching on. Worms are the worst. Worms are like, I don't know, junior-varsity snakes. No, don't look at me like that. They really are."

"You're not exactly Mr. Outdoors, are you?" Robbie said. "Not exactly Mr. One-with-Nature."

Marty stared at the fish again and made a face. "Whatever. Just take it off!" he said, a hint of panic in his voice. "Please!"

It was the afternoon following the Yankees game, and after finishing their homework, the two boys had grabbed their fishing rods and headed to the big pond on the other side of the neighborhood. Robbie had just finished telling Marty about his encounter with Ben when Marty felt a tug on the line and reeled in the bluegill.

But it wasn't until Robbie unhooked it and threw it back in the pond, where it darted away, that Marty could concentrate on the story again.

"Whew," Marty said. "Okay, back to the one-armed kid. Tell me the truth: was he kind of creepy?"

"No way," Robbie said, casting his line again. "He seems like a regular kid. A regular kid who went through something terrible, something most of us could never imagine happening."

"I've never seen a kid run that fast," Marty said. "The dude can motor! I'm surprised you caught up to him."

"I was, too," Robbie said. "He looked gassed when we

stopped. But maybe he sort of *wanted* to be caught."

"Why would he want that?"

"I don't know," Robbie said. "Just a theory. Maybe he's lonely. Maybe he just moved here and he needs some friends."

"Boy, that would be tough," Marty said. "Being the new kid and having only one arm." He baited his hook with another piece of hot dog and cast his line again. "And he used to play baseball?"

Robbie nodded. "That's what he told me. I bet he was a shortstop. You can see how athletic he is. Probably has a sick arm too."

"Speaking of sick," Marty said, "I'll tell you who's *really* sick: Big Red. As in, sick in the head."

Big Red! With all the excitement over chasing Ben and finally getting to talk to him, Robbie had forgotten all about the hulking Yankees pitcher and his postgame woofing with Marty.

"Did you two had a nice conversation after I left?" Robbie said.

Marty turned pale again. "He said he'd pound my face in next time he saw me."

"I don't think he could do it—even with all those muscles," Robbie said, grinning. "My money's on you. You're too quick for him. Just bob and weave. Stay low to the ground. Oh, wait. You already *are* low to the ground."

"Thanks for the vote of confidence," Marty said. "Maybe he'll forget about me by the time we play them again."

"Doubtful," Robbie said. "We play the Yankees in two weeks. Last game of the season, remember?"

Marty groaned. "That's it, I'm a dead man! D-E-A-D! And I'm an only child. Well, except for my brother."

"Look on the bright side," Robbie said. "If you're dead, you won't have to take the Vulture's English final."

The Vulture was Ms. Patricia Owens, one of the most feared teachers at York Middle, a woman who was said to have worn a perpetual scowl since birth.

She was nicknamed the Vulture for her unnerving habit of lazily circling the room during oral quizzes, and swooping down on the poor kid who gave a wrong answer, soundly embarrassing him or her.

When you made a mistake in the Vulture's class, you were said to be "roadkill." Unfortunately, Robbie was intimately familiar with the experience, having been singled out by the Vulture several times.

"You're killing me, dude," Marty said. "Aren't you supposed to be my friend? Aren't you supposed to offer encouragement at times like this?"

Robbie clapped him on the back and said, "Aw, I'm just playing with you. Big Red's forgotten all about you already. Are you kidding? With his sunny personality, he probably threatens twenty kids every day before lunch. How do you expect a guy like that to keep track of all the kids he wants to pound?"

Marty shook his head sadly. "I guess that's supposed to make me feel better. But somehow it doesn't."

For the next few minutes, neither boy spoke. The sun had disappeared behind a cloud and the water looked more green than blue, with large shadows forming in the tree line where they stood.

"I hope Ben shows up at practice Thursday," Robbie said finally. "I have an idea. I mentioned it to Dad last night when I got home."

"What's your idea?"

"Uh-uh," Robbie said. "If I tell you, it'll end up on Facebook five minutes later."

Marty was genuinely shocked. "Me?" he said. "Dude, I am the soul of discretion! I should work for the CIA, I'm so good with secrets!"

"No offense," Robbie said, "but you're actually the biggest blabbermouth I know."

"Fine, be like that," Marty said in a pouty voice.

Suddenly there was a tug on his line. Marty reeled in furiously and another bluegill broke the surface, twisting and turning. This one was much larger than the first.

"Oh, great!" he moaned, clearly imagining another unhooking ordeal. "How come I'm the only one catching fish?"

Robbie laughed and clapped him on the back.

"Just your lucky day, I guess."

Robbie was the first player to arrive at practice. This was nothing unusual. Ray Hammond had long stressed the idea of punctuality to his three children. Only in Ray's case, punctuality meant showing up at least a half-hour early for any appointment or function.

Arriving only fifteen minutes early actually meant you were late, according to him. And arriving on time meant you were very, *very* late. Robbie, Jackie, and Ashley had never quite gotten used to what they called DWT (Dad Weirdo Time), but none of them could recall ever being late for anything in their lives.

As soon as the black Ford pickup came to a stop, Robbie jumped out and anxiously scanned the field. He checked the backstop, then down the first base and third base lines.

No Ben.

He looked out toward center field and the old score-board behind the fence, then beyond to the trees that partially obscured the pool. But Ben was nowhere in sight.

Disappointed, Robbie reached into the truck bed and helped his dad unload the equipment bags that held the bases, the catcher's gear, baseballs, and bats. They pulled out the cooler with the water bottles, too, and carried or dragged everything across the dusty field to one of the dugouts.

"Where you been?" a voice said.

It was Ben.

He sat at the far end of the dugout wearing an orange T-shirt, basketball shorts and flip-flops, and the same Orioles hat, the brim facing forward this time. On his left hand was a battered black glove.

"Ben!" Robbie said. "We weren't sure you'd—"

Ben grinned nervously and looked at Robbie's dad.

"Thought you might need someone to shag balls," he said. "Y'know, during batting practice or something. But it's cool if you don't. I'll get out of your way and watch from the stands."

Ray Hammond smiled and put down his bag. "Nice to meet you, Ben," he said. "Robbie told me a lot about you. We'd love to have you join us." The coach peered at the boy's feet. "But I'd prefer that you play in sneakers. Do you have—"

Robbie cut him off. "I'm sure it'll be okay, just for today." He gave his father a look that said, *Don't ruin this.* "Right, Dad?"

Coach got the message. "Right, just for today. Why don't you two go warm up?"

Ben's face lit up. Robbie grabbed his glove and a ball, and the two boys jogged down the line to play catch.

Just as Robbie had suspected, Ben was a natural athlete. He threw with a smooth, practiced motion, the ball popping into Robbie's glove with a loud *whump!* And Ben caught the ball effortlessly, too, guiding the glove easily, no matter where the throw reached him.

It was in-between his catch and throw that he struggled.

After every catch, he would place the glove under the stump of his right arm and then attempt to pull the ball out. It was an awkward, time-consuming movement. He fumbled with the exchange and dropped both the glove and the ball several times, appearing to grow frustrated.

"Sorry," he mumbled. "Haven't done this much. Practiced a little at home with my mom. Obviously, I don't have it down yet."

But Robbie didn't mind. It was great to see Ben playing ball—any kind of ball—after all the kid had been through. And it was great to see the delighted look on his face as he became more and more comfortable popping the ball out of his glove for the return throw.

Soon the rest of the Orioles began arriving. Robbie introduced Ben to each of them. They crowded around him, obviously still in awe of what the one-armed kid had done at their last practice.

"Dude," Joey said, "that catch of yours was *SportsCenter* stuff! Should've made their highlights!"

"We saw your wheels, too," Willie said. "Wish you could be our designated base-stealer!"

"Uh, thanks," Ben said, looking down, his face reddening.

"Yeah," Jordy said, "even in flip-flops, you're way faster than any of us."

"In fact, you could run backward in those things and be faster than Marty," Connor added as the rest of the Orioles cracked up.

"Ha, ha, ha, you guys are hysterical," Marty said. He pushed his way through the other players until he was next to Ben.

"Mr. Ben Landrum," he began, "let me just say how honored we are to have you visit our humble little practice. It's certainly a privilege to be able to stand here and—"

Now the Orioles stuck their fingers in their mouths and made gagging sounds.

"Marty, ease up," Robbie said. "He's not the president of the United States."

"Or the head of the Supreme Court," Mike added.

"And if you saw my report card, you know I never will be," Ben said, touching off more laughter.

"Oh?" Marty said. "An underachiever, eh? Well, if you ever need help with schoolwork, come to me. Don't go to any of these losers. These guys couldn't spell *cat* if you spotted them the *C*, the *A*, *and* the *T*."

At this, the Orioles began booing and pummeling Marty with their gloves until he ran away to escape.

A moment later, Robbie's dad looked at the knot of players and grinned. "Ben, what're you doing, signing autographs over there?" he said. "Let's go, guys. Leave him alone and go get loose so we can start practice."

It turned out to be one of the best practices the Orioles had had all season. Even though the day was sunny, it was unseasonably cool for early June. And whether it was the seventy-degree temperature that was energizing them or simply Ben's presence, the Orioles looked more focused than they had in weeks.

For his part, Ben was all over the field.

At first he watched the Orioles take infield for a few minutes. Then he stood behind Robbie and Mike on the sidelines, quietly observing as each threw twenty or so pitches to Joey, working on control. As Coach pitched batting practice, Ben shagged fly balls in the outfield, jogging easily in his flip-flops and making graceful basket catches of almost every ball hit to him.

"Dude's played the game," Willie said to Robbie at one point.

"Oh, yeah," Robbie said. "He was giving Marty tips out there about positioning. And how to stand when the pitcher throws a certain pitch."

Willie grunted. "That's a good thing," he said. "Marty needs all the tips he can get."

"Now, now," Robbie said. "Marty's improving. . . ."

"You could have fooled me," Willie said with a smirk. "Personally, my tip to the boy would be: Try lacrosse, you might like it."

"You are a cruel, cruel kid, Willie Pitts," Robbie said, trotting off the field. "Luckily, I don't have to listen to this anymore. My turn to hit next."

Forty-five minutes later, after all the Orioles had batted, Coach Hammond waved to the newest player.

"Ben!" he shouted. "You're up!"

The boy's eyes widened with surprise. Then he frowned and shook his head.

"Thanks, Coach!" he shouted. "I'm good!"

"Uh-uh," Coach said, still waving. "You practice, you hit. That's the rule."

Reluctantly, Ben jogged in. He grabbed a bat and trudged to the plate, aware that all eyes were on him.

Holding the bat high, he took a few awkward practice swings and stepped in. Coach threw him a belt-high fastball. He swung viciously and missed. He whiffed on the next pitch and the next pitch and the one after that, too.

After swinging and missing the fifth pitch, Ben tomahawked the bat on the plate in frustration. The Orioles stole nervous glances at each other. Coach had a cardinal rule: no drama. Ever. No temper tantrums when things go wrong. No throwing gloves when a ground ball goes between your legs. No throwing bats when you strike out.

But all Coach said to Ben now was, "Relax. Take a deep breath. Nice level swing. You'll make contact. Just like you used to."

Which is exactly what happened.

It was nothing much, a routine grounder to second base that Willie gobbled up easily. But the Orioles could see the relief on Ben's face. And after a few more pitches, he smoothed out his choppy, upward swing enough to lash a line drive.

When practice was over, Robbie and his dad watched as Ben and Marty ran to the outfield, throwing fly balls to each other and laughing as they tried to catch them behind their backs.

"Ben's going to play ball again," Robbie said quietly. "I just know he is."

His dad nodded. "I think you're right," he said. "This

season's almost over. But maybe next year. Which wouldn't be the worst thing. Give him a whole year to work on that move. You know, getting the ball out of the glove."

He rubbed his chin for a moment, a thoughtful look on his face.

"In the meantime," he continued, "we may have found ourselves a great assistant coach."

19

The Hammonds' backyard bustled with activity. It was late Saturday afternoon, and Robbie's dad was firing up the grill. His mom was unwrapping a platter of hamburgers and hot dogs. Robbie and Ashley were setting the patio table. Ben was due to arrive any minute for a cookout, during which Ray Hammond planned to ask him if he'd help coach the Orioles.

"It's like that old line from the mob movie: 'I'll make him an offer he can't refuse,'" his dad had joked earlier. "A free snowball after every game! With marshmallow topping! How can you turn down a deal like that?"

Right now, though, Robbie was going over what he called "the Ben Ground Rules" for Ashley.

"Don't ask about his missing arm," Robbie said.

Ashley made an elaborate show of yawning. It was her favorite way of expressing major disinterest.

"And don't stare at his missing arm, either."

Ashley rolled her eyes.

"That's dumb," she said. "How can I stare at something that's missing? Do you stare at the missing roller coaster back here? Or the missing Lexus in the driveway?"

"You know what I mean," Robbie said. "Just don't . . . *look* at him too much."

"Okay," she said. She threw her head back until she was staring up at the sky. "How's this? I'll stay like this the whole time. 'What's that, Ben? Oh, were you talking to me? Sorry, I didn't know. Because I'm not supposed to look at you.'"

She pretended to munch on a burger. "Hmmm, might be hard to eat in this position. Oh well, if I choke to death, just roll my body under the table. I wouldn't want to make your precious Ben feel uncomfortable."

Robbie grinned. Ashley could be like Marty when she got on a roll. Or Mr. Rumsey. There was no stopping her until she ran out of snappy things to say. Only then would the act be over.

"I know, why don't we *all* stare up at the sky while Ben's here!" she said. "That won't make him feel too self-conscious."

"Okay, okay," Robbie said, throwing up his hands and laughing. "You win. Just don't do anything crazy."

"That's me, Crazy Ashley. Don't worry, I won't embarrass you," she said. "Besides, I bet he's not nearly as wacko about his missing arm as you are."

At precisely five p.m., the doorbell rang. There on the front steps was Ben. Next to him was a stressed-looking woman who introduced herself as Ben's mom, Beth Landrum.

"Won't you join us for dinner, Beth?" Robbie's mom asked.

Mrs. Landrum smiled and shook her head. "Thanks, but I'm off to work," she said. "On weekends I wait tables downtown. And I'm running late. Could you drop Ben at home later? His older sister will watch him." She kissed Ben on the forehead, waved, and hurried back to her car.

No sooner had the door closed than Mary Hammond started in. "Ben, I hear you're a pretty good athlete," she said. "Ever play cornhole—you know, with the beanbags? We'll play after dinner. Although you don't want to play *me*, buster. I never lose. *Ever.* Ask Robbie. I'll beat you like a drum."

Robbie looked at Ben and shook his head slowly. Well, he thought, that didn't take long. In fact, he was pretty sure this was a new personal record for his mom: trash-talking someone she'd known for all of ten seconds.

But Ben just laughed and said, "Cornhole?! I will *own you up*, Mrs. Hammond! Heck, I haven't lost at that since I was, like, two."

Dueling trash-talkers, Robbie thought. Could be an interesting cookout. It'll *definitely* be an interesting corn-hole game.

When they sat down to eat a few minutes later, Ben told Robbie and his family all about himself. He and his mom and his older sister, Bernadette, had moved to Baltimore from New Jersey three months ago. His mom, he explained, was looking for a fresh start and had taken a job teaching kindergarten at a private school.

"Our old house had too many bad memories for her," he said. "The divorce, my accident, Bernie having problems in school . . ."

Now, Ben said, they were living in an apartment across town and Bernie was going to the high school nearby, where her attitude and grades were already much better. And he was attending the middle school there, although he hoped to transfer to York Middle next fall, when the Landrums would be moving into a new house.

Seconds later, he turned to Ashley and smiled. "Robbie gave you all the gory details about my arm, right?" he asked. "What else you wanna know? The tiger that chewed it off? Man, he was huge!"

"Oh, Ben," Robbie said as Ashley giggled. "You don't have to—"

Ben held up his hand. "No, it's okay," he said. "All the questions from strangers, that gets old. But you guys are friends."

Ashley shot Robbie a triumphant look. For the next few minutes, Ben patiently answered every question she fired at him. He talked about his long stay in the hospital after the accident, about the months and months of rehabilitation, about all the things he had to learn to do with one arm, simple things like putting on socks and buckling a seat belt that weren't so simple anymore.

Ashley hung on every word.

"I still have 'phantom pain' every once in a while," Ben said.

"Phantom pain?" she repeated. "What's that?"

"It's pain you feel where the arm has been amputated," he said. "The doctors said that even though the arm isn't there, the nerves where it was cut off still send pain signals to the brain. And somehow they make the brain think the arm is still there."

"Okay, Miss Ashley," Robbie's dad said finally. "Give Ben a break with the questions."

"Fine," she said, picking up her plate and pushing away from the table. "I'm full, anyway. Nice meeting you. But I can see the boys want to talk about something else. Oh, and by the way? They're going to ask if you'll help coach their dumb old baseball team."

As Robbie and his dad stared openmouthed at Ashley, Mary Hammond laughed.

"As you see, there aren't exactly any secrets in this house," she said as Ashley ran off.

Now it was Ben's turn to look surprised.

"How about it, Ben?" Robbie's dad said. "The Orioles need an assistant coach. I could use the help. All the players like you, and everyone can see you know the game. It'll give us a fresh set of eyes on some of the problem areas that need fixing."

Ben said nothing for a moment. He looked at each of them in turn, as if trying to decide if they were joking. "Okay, sure," he said finally, a little dazed. "That would be awesome."

Mary Hammond clapped with delight. "We'll celebrate with ice cream for dessert!" she said. Then she nodded her head in the direction of the cornhole set in the yard and pointed to Ben. "But first, you and I have a little business to take care of, mister."

"Absolutely!" Ben said, leaping to his feet. "Tell you

what, Mrs. H., I'll even give you a break and play lefty."

He started laughing so hard that within seconds Robbie and his mom and dad were laughing along with him.

The cornhole game was close from beginning to end. Robbie's mom was a whiz at the game, but Ben turned out to be a terrific player, too. And he had a unique style, windmilling his arm and making the beanbag float high in the air—higher than Robbie had ever seen anyone toss it—before it landed with a thud near the target hole.

"Are you playing cornhole, or trying to hit the Space Station?" Mary Hammond said at one point, trying to get Ben off his game with her usual nonstop chatter.

"Scoreboard! Scoreboard!" Ben chanted. "I believe you're down sixteen–thirteen, right? Soon as I whup you, I'll give you a lesson on how to throw like this."

"No thanks, hotshot," Robbie's mom said. "The patented Mary Hammond low-elevation toss has worked for years. It's the one that's going to land me in the Cornhole Hall of Fame—if there *is* such a thing."

"If there is," said Ben, grinning, "I'll probably have my own wing." He fired the beanbag high in the air—his highest toss yet—and this time it dropped cleanly in the hole.

"Aaahhh!" Robbie's mom said with a strangled cry. "You're so lucky, you know that?"

Ben shrugged nonchalantly. "Another day, another winning toss," he said, yawning for good measure.

In the end, it was Ben who made good on all his trash-talking, squeaking out a 21–19 win that left Mary Hammond howling in mock pain.

It was one of the few times Robbie ever saw his mom

lose at cornhole, but it was clear from the way she was laughing and high-fiving Ben that she didn't mind at all.

A few minutes later, they were back on the patio enjoying homemade chocolate ice cream.

"This is the most fun I've had in a long time," Ben said quietly. "I almost forgot what it's like."

It was still light out, so after dessert, Robbie got two gloves and the boys played catch. Robbie could see that Ben was looking more and more comfortable flipping the ball out of the glove for the return throw. They played until it was almost too dark to see, even when they threw the ball high in the sky to catch the last faint patches of light.

"Know the first thing I'm going to do as the Orioles assistant coach?" Ben asked.

"Get yourself some sneakers?" Robbie teased.

Ben didn't miss a beat. "Okay, the *second* thing I'm going to do. I'm going to get you straightened out."

Robbie sighed and thought: *Good luck with that plan.*

"Dude," Ben said, "you've got one of the best arms I've ever seen. What I don't get is: why did you suck like you did against the Yankees? To give up three runs? To those losers? With your stuff? That's just pathetic."

Robbie felt as if he'd been slapped. *Pathetic?* Had Ben really used that word to describe his pitching?

Robbie could feel tears welling in his eyes—he was glad it was too dark for Ben to notice. No, it wouldn't be cool for the Orioles new assistant coach to see him crying. Robbie knew his voice would be shaky, too. So he didn't say anything, trying to get his emotions under control first.

"No offense," Ben continued, and Robbie winced. Because whenever anyone started a sentence with *no offense*, it usually meant whatever followed was going to offend the other person, big-time. "But you were pretty awful out there. Is something wrong with your arm?"

More like my head, Robbie thought, choking back a sob.

Then it all came out, in a torrent of words he couldn't stop if he tried.

Sitting there in the darkness, he told Ben all about last year's all-star game. About how big and strong and confident Stevie Altman had looked as he stepped into the batter's box. About the fastball that got away, the hardest pitch he had ever thrown. About how it crashed into

Stevie's batting helmet, right at the temple, and how Stevie had dropped as if he'd been shot.

Robbie's voice was cracking now, and he was sniffling, too. But he didn't care. After months of keeping all this inside, it felt good to let it out—especially to someone his own age.

He even told Ben about his recurring dream—okay, it was more like a nightmare—where the ball was headed straight toward Stevie's head, and the boy didn't even try to get out of the way. He just got this strange look on his face, closed his eyes, and mouthed silently, "Here it comes."

Ben listened without interrupting. When Robbie finished, the only sound was the low buzzing of the night's insects.

"Wow," Ben said finally. "That must have been pretty awful."

Robbie wiped his eyes. "Now I don't trust my control. Not when I throw hard, anyway. And you saw what happens when I lob it in there."

"I saw," Ben said. "That shot Big Red hit—it hasn't come down yet."

Robbie managed a weak chuckle.

"My old coach used to call that a room-service fastball," Ben said. "'Cause you delivered it to the batter on a silver platter."

"Yep," Robbie said. "Only thing I didn't do was shout, 'Come and get it!'" He shivered lightly in the damp air. "But I don't ever want to hit another batter, I can tell you that."

Someone inside switched on the patio light. Robbie could see Ben nodding now, appearing lost in thought.

"So somehow we have to get you past this beaning. . . ." he said.

"Ugh," Robbie said. "Do you have to use that word? Sounds so . . . *harsh*."

"Fine," Ben said with a grin. "Somehow we have to get you past the incident where you caused a horsehide spheroid to engage with the skull of another young athlete. Accidentally, of course."

"Okay, go back to *beaning*," Robbie said. "Because now you sound like Marty."

"What's weird is that you realize it wasn't intentional, just a terrible accident," Ben went on. "And yet you're still afraid you'll hit someone. . . ."

"It's like I can't forget it," Robbie blurted.

"That's okay; you might *never* forget it," Ben said. "I don't think I'll ever forget that day in the woods. And the bike coming down on me. I remember everything about it. Even how blue the sky looked as the bike tore into me."

Ben shook his head, as if trying to erase the thought.

"But you—you can't let this hold you back forever," he continued. "It took a long time for me to move on. Now we have to figure out what it'll take for you to do it."

"It's not like I haven't tried," Robbie said. "My mom and dad say to give it time. But it's been almost a year. I'm tired of pitching like crap. Not having a clue about where the ball's going when it leaves my hand. And the other teams laughing at me." He snorted. "Heck, my own teammates were laughing at me until a few weeks ago. They were calling me Ball Four."

Ben nodded. "Bet that hurt," he said. "But so much of

control is about confidence. We have to get you back to throwing the way you did before you plunked that kid." He shot Robbie a look. "How about *plunked*? Is *plunked* all right?"

Robbie sighed wearily. "Sure. Plunked is fine. Whatever."

Ben stared off into the darkness for a moment.

"Okay, let's try something," he said suddenly. "No game Tuesday, right?"

"Right," Robbie said. "We're off. And we play the Rays Friday."

"Let's get a few of the guys and meet at the practice field Tuesday," Ben said. "Get your buddy Marty. And we need a catcher, so Joey has to be there. Maybe a couple of other guys to shag balls, too."

"You have an idea?"

"Maybe," Ben said. "We're going to have a batter stand in against you. And you're going to throw hard. Like you used to. And you're going to do that over and over again until you're comfortable. Until you know you can do it."

"Ha!" Robbie said. "Like anyone on the Orioles would ever stand there! Those guys know how wild I am. I almost took Willie's head off in batting practice one day. And I just missed Jordy's kneecap with another pitch. Marty, he'd rather be tossed into a pit with five hundred rattlesnakes than hit against me."

Robbie looked down. "No, no way," he continued sadly. "Who's crazy enough to step in against a scatter-armed twelve-year-old head case?"

Ben didn't hesitate.

"Me," was all he said.

It was ninety-five degrees with not a hint of a breeze, and Joey was in full whine mode.

"Tell me again why we're doing this?" he said, snapping on his shin guards. "On the single hottest day of the year?"

Robbie was asking himself the same thing. It was one of those afternoons when the infield felt like concrete in the baking sun, and heat waves shimmered off the outfield grass. The sounds of splashing and laughing at the pool were already driving them crazy, and they had only been there ten minutes.

Along with Robbie, Joey, and Ben, three other Orioles were on hand for the great Help-Robbie-Get-His-Control-Back Experiment: Gabe, Yancy, and Marty. And it was not helping Joey's mood that Marty kept trying to engage him in conversation.

"You know what they call the catcher's equipment, right?" Marty said as Joey pulled on his chest protector.

Joey sighed and wiped his face with the neck of his T-shirt. "No, Marty, I don't. But I'm sure you're about to tell me."

"They call it 'the tools of ignorance,'" Marty said. "That's absolutely true. Google it if you don't believe me."

Joey narrowed his eyes, but said nothing.

"And you know why they call it that?" Marty went on. "Because of all the punishment a catcher takes. In other words, you have to be sort of ignorant—now don't get all mad, Joey—to want to play the position."

Joey spit in his catcher's mitt and slowly rubbed the saliva into the pocket. Then he pulled on his mask, peered at Marty, and said, "I have no freakin' idea what you're talking about."

Marty turned to the others with outstretched arms. "Gentlemen of the jury," he said with a grin, "I rest my case."

The rest of the Orioles cracked up. No matter what the occasion, even on the most brutal of summer days, Marty could always be counted on for comic relief.

"All right, let's get going," Ben said, picking up a bat. "Robbie, loosen that arm for a minute. Then we'll start."

"It's seven thousand degrees out here," Joey said, squatting behind the plate. "Does he really need to warm up?"

"Uh, *yeah*, he does," Ben said. "Unless you want to see him hurt his arm. Or his shoulder. We want him throwing hard today."

Robbie threw easily in warm-ups, his arm feeling loose from the start, probably because of the weather. By his seventh or eighth throw, the ball was popping into Joey's mitt and rocking the big catcher's hand back. Robbie signaled that he was ready, and Ben stepped into the batter's box.

True to his word, Ben had worn sneakers instead of flip-flops today. He furiously carved a trough with his back foot. When he was through, he stepped in close to the plate, held the bat high with his left hand, and waggled it.

"Okay, bring it!" he said.

Robbie felt weird staring in at a one-armed batter. He took a deep breath and murmured, "Okay, you can do this." He was just about to go into his windup when Ben suddenly smiled and stepped out.

"Oh, one thing," Ben shouted. "Whatever you do, don't hit me in the right arm. 'Cause that would really hurt!"

Robbie groaned, and the other Orioles seemed a little uncomfortable. Joey pushed up his face mask and gave Ben a perplexed look.

"A little amputee humor there," Ben said.

"Oh," Joey said, nodding slowly. "Okay, now I get it." He pulled the mask back down and went into his crouch again.

Robbie's first few pitches were low and outside, as they often seemed to be when he faced a live batter. He stepped off the rubber and walked around the mound talking to himself again.

"Don't think, throw!" Ben said. "And I *know* you can throw harder than that!"

But Robbie wasn't sure he could. Not with Ben crowding the plate even more than most batters, practically leaning over it. The kid was almost begging to be hit!

All sorts of thoughts flashed through Robbie's head. What if he nailed Ben, this open, funny kid who had become such a good friend in just a few days, a kid who had already been through hell?

It would be like: Welcome to Baltimore, kid. Here's a fastball in the ribs to remember us by. Or, worse, a heater to the head that smacks you so hard you won't remember anything.

Robbie felt the familiar faint trembling in his legs now. His chest was pounding, too, and he could feel his right hand sweating the way it always did—even in cool weather—when he faced a batter.

"Throw!" Ben shouted.

"C'mon, dude!" Marty shouted from the outfield. "You can do it!"

"Are you gonna pitch, or what?" Joey yelled. "It's hot out here!"

Okay, Robbie thought. You asked for it. All of you.

He went into his windup, kicked high, and fired. Oh God, he thought, it's headed straight for his head!

Except . . . no, it really wasn't. It was a rocket, high and inside. And Ben easily ducked out of the way as it slammed into Joey's glove.

"Better!" Ben said, grinning. "That had something on it! Again!"

Only when he was sure he had missed Ben did Robbie dare to exhale. He felt light-headed now, and his legs were shaking. Throw like that *again*? He felt like he was going to pass out. But somehow he willed himself to go into his windup and fire again.

"Watch out!" he cried, his voice shrill and panicky, convinced the pitch was headed for Ben again. But this one was low and inside, and Ben watched as it, too, plunked harmlessly into Joey's mitt.

"Okay!" Ben said now, stepping out. "Two pretty good fastballs! And I'm still alive! See? You can do this!"

Probably not without puking, Robbie thought, his stomach roiling. But again and again and again, he forced himself to throw. One pitch went completely behind Ben. One sailed over his head and clanged into the backstop. A few skipped in the dirt and were smothered by Joey. But quite a few were around the plate, tantalizing enough for most hitters to swing at.

Finally, after ten minutes, Robbie waved his arms and said, "That's it, I'm done." He was exhausted now, his breath coming in gasps.

"Okay," Ben said. He dropped the bat and signaled to the others to come in. Then he jogged out to Robbie and gave him a fist bump. "I know that was hard. But I think you made major progress."

"I . . . *guess*," Robbie said, staggering toward the dugout. "I need to sit down."

One by one, the others joined him to get out of the scorching sun. They cracked their water bottles and drank greedily.

"I think you're getting there, dude," Marty said. "Threw some strikes today. Remember: 'Progress lies not in enhancing what is, but in advancing toward what will be.'"

They all stared at him.

"What?" he said. "You never heard that? From Khalil Gibran? Famous Lebanese American poet?"

Still no one spoke. They continued to stare.

Finally Gabe said: "Tell the truth, Marty. What planet are you from?"

A few minutes later, as they began gathering up their

equipment, Yancy said, "Here's a radical idea. I say we hit the pool."

"Excellent!" Ben said. "And you guys are in for a treat. I'm about to show you my famous one-armed butterfly stroke."

Joey stopped and looked at him. "But how can you do the butterfly with just one . . . ohhhh, another joke," he said. "I get it now."

Marty looked at the others and rolled his eyes.

"Sure you do, Joey," he said, clapping the big guy on the back. "Sure you do."

Ray Hammond gathered the Orioles in the dugout twenty minutes before they were to take the field against the Rays.

"Men," Coach said, "here we are, down to our final two games of the season. And we intend to win both of them, don't we?"

The Orioles were like bobbleheads again, smiling and nodding vigorously.

"Because we never quit, do we? Never, ever."

On cue, the bobbleheads frowned and shook their heads.

"Good," Coach said. "And this young man right here, Ben Landrum, is going to help us. I've asked him to be our new assistant coach. Some of you know he's already been working with Robbie. Now he's going to be working with all of you."

Marty shot his hand in the air and cried, "Oooh, oooh, oooh!"

"Marty," Coach said, "you're not in a classroom. You don't have to raise your hand to speak."

Marty stood and pointed to Ben. "Do we have to call you Coach now?"

"Absolutely not," Ben said, grinning. "A simple Your Majesty will do. Or Sir Ben. Either one is fine."

The Orioles cracked up, hooting and whistling until Coach told them to pipe down.

"Now," Coach continued, "even though it's been a long and difficult—"

Marty's hand went up again.

Coach sighed. "Yes, Marty?"

"Quick question, Coach. Are we still in last place?"

Now Willie jumped to his feet and said, "Hmmm, lemme check the standings. . . ." He pretended to open a newspaper and scan down the page with his index finger. "Here we are," he said at last. "It says, 'Orioles, oh and ten.' Oh, wait, it says something else, too: 'Crappiest team in the league.' So, yeah. I'm pretty sure we're in last place."

"What about the Blue Jays?" Jordy said. "Those losers can't be ahead of us, can they?"

"Those losers are only semi-losers now," Connor said. "They actually have two wins. Somehow they beat the Red Sox."

"Whole Red Sox team must've come down with the flu," Mike muttered. "Because the Blue Jays *really* suck."

"Which means we must suck worse," Willie said. "Do I have to remind you they beat us?"

"Okay, okay," Coach said, raising his hands for quiet. "Enough with the gloom and doom. Didn't we just say we never give up? Now we're down to a two-game season. That's how we're going to look at it. Two games: Rays and Yankees. And we can take them both."

Marty looked at Robbie and whispered, "I don't know . . . Big Red's pretty tough."

"We can beat Big Red!" Ben said, staring fiercely at Marty. "He's good, but nowhere near as good as he thinks he is. Plus he's an all-world tool."

The Orioles chuckled and nodded.

"You'll get no arguments from us, Sir Ben!" Marty sang out.

"All right, but let's think about the Yankees later," Coach said. He pointed at the Rays, who had just finished taking infield. "Right now we need to concentrate on those guys. They're all that matters. Maybe we're not going to the play-offs, but our second season begins right now. In fact, that's our new motto."

The Orioles looked at each other and exchanged fist bumps and glove taps, getting psyched.

Coach clapped and said, "Let's go, hands in the middle. Second season on three."

The Orioles clambered to their feet. "One, two, three . . . second season!" they shouted.

Right before they took the field, Robbie felt a hand on his shoulder. It was Ben. He started to say something, but Robbie cut him off.

"I know, I know . . . throw hard, right? Throw like I did the other day to you. Pretend it's just me and Joey out there."

Ben grinned. "Wow," he said. "My first game coaching and I'm that predictable, huh?"

Robbie shook his head. "It's not that," he said. "It's that

I shouldn't need anyone to tell me. I should've been doing that all along. But thanks, anyway."

When the first Rays batter stepped in, a tall kid batting from the left side of the plate, Robbie was surprised. His right hand wasn't sweating as much as it normally did. He could feel his heart thumping, but it wasn't pounding like a bass drum.

There was no question he felt better about his control after the last throwing session with Ben.

Not a whole lot better. Not great.

Just . . . better.

Okay, he thought, here we go. No grandma fastballs. No room-service stuff served on a rolling cart so they can smack it into the next zip code.

Nothing but hard stuff.

Joey put down one finger. Fastball. He wanted it low. Robbie nodded and went into his windup.

The pitch felt good leaving his hand, like it was going where he wanted it to. Now it tailed inside, but Robbie wasn't alarmed, not at first. Then it was too late to cry out.

It caught the batter on his right thigh.

The kid went down hard, wincing in pain, the bat flying behind him.

Robbie stared in disbelief. It felt like a dream—a really bad dream. *First pitch and I hit a kid? No way!*

Now the Rays coach was running to his batter while shouting at Ray Hammond, "Is that what you teach your guys, Coach? Throw at the first kid? Intimidate the other team from the get-go?"

But the Rays batter climbed to his feet right away and quickly trotted down to first base. And while Robbie's dad tried to reassure the other coach that no one was throwing at the Rays intentionally, Ben paid a visit to the mound.

"Okay," he said, "one got away from you. But the kid's fine. You can see he's fine, right?"

Robbie checked out the runner on first. Then he looked back at Ben and nodded numbly.

"The kid's not even *rubbing* where you hit him!" Ben continued. "So you didn't exactly cripple him. Just nicked him, is all."

It was true. The kid was smiling now, chatting with the first base coach as if nothing had happened and they were discussing their favorite TV show.

"So now you have to shake it off," Ben went on. "I know that's tough to do. But you gotta move on. Like we talked about, like I had to do after the accident. And the only way for you to move on is throw hard. And prove to yourself you can get guys out."

Ben smacked him on the shoulder and left. As the next batter dug in, Robbie took a deep breath. His legs felt unsteady and his hands were still trembling. But I'm not giving in, he thought. Ben was right. If he ever hoped to get back his old form, he had to throw heat.

And he did.

But it wasn't pretty.

Four straight balls to the Rays' number two hitter put runners on first and second. With the count 3 and 2, the next batter swung at a high fastball—a pitch he couldn't have reached with a stepladder—for the first out. Robbie walked the next batter to load the bases. Then the Rays number five hitter crossed them up and laid down a bunt that Joey pounced on, except his throw to first sailed over Jordy's head as two runs crossed the plate.

"My bad all the way," Joey said, kicking at the dirt in disgust.

"It's okay," Robbie said. That was something he had always admired about Joey. The kid might be a rock head, but he never made excuses, always manned up when he made an error or screwed up an at-bat.

Still throwing hard, Robbie promptly walked the next kid. But each of the next two batters helped him out big-time, swinging at terrible pitches in the dirt for back-to-back strikeouts to end the inning.

Robbie trudged back to the dugout with his head down. Score after one inning: Rays 2, Orioles 0. And everyone in the ballpark knew the Orioles were lucky to be trailing only by two.

"Okay," Ben said. "You're all over the place. But at least you're throwing hard. That's the first step, right? Now we get some runs. Then you go back out there and shut them down."

"You make it sound so *easy*!" Robbie barked, and right away he was sorry to lash out at his new friend. But Ben seemed to take it in stride.

"No," he said evenly. "It's not easy. Not easy at all. But I *know* you can do it."

As Ben had predicted, the Orioles got some runs. Willie led off with a single and scored on a double by Jordy. After Connor flied out to center, Carlos delivered a run-scoring single to tie the game before Riley hit a line drive to the Rays' first baseman, who stepped on the bag to double up Carlos and end the inning.

Still, now it was Rays 2, Orioles 2.

Just like that, the Orioles had new life.

"There you go, big guy!" Ben said before Robbie took the mound again. "We're back in the game! Now keep us there."

Only, things got even worse for Robbie in the second inning.

He walked the first two batters on eight straight pitches, not one even close to a strike. And his first pitch to the next Rays hitter rocketed over the kid's head and clanged ten feet up the backstop. Even the umpire whipped off his mask and turned around to see where the ball hit, smiling in amusement.

Then Robbie heard it.

Heck, everybody heard it. They could probably hear it in Alaska. It came from the Rays dugout, a sound he recognized right away.

They were singing "Wild Thing," that dumb song in the *Major League* movies that he and his dad still watched occasionally. The song the Cleveland Indians crowd sings when the crazy-wild relief pitcher with the thick ugly glasses—what was his name, Ricky Vaughn?—comes into the game:

Wild Thing, you make my heart sing. . . .

Robbie looked at the stands. Little kids were standing and pointing at him and laughing. Moms and dads were shaking their heads at the song and exchanging knowing looks. Even the Rays batter was smirking as the serenade continued.

Robbie tugged at the brim of his cap, pulled it down low so no one could see the tears welling in his eyes.

Then he picked up the rosin bag and slammed it down angrily. Nice job, jerk face, he thought. Way to come through for your team. Two games left and you have the biggest meltdown of the season!

Seconds later, Ray Hammond popped out of the dugout and walked slowly to the mound, signaling for Mike to come on in relief.

"Sorry, son," his dad said, holding out his right hand for the ball. "You didn't have it today. But we're still in this one. And I owe it to the team to try to win it."

The walk to the dugout felt like the longest walk of Robbie's life. He slumped dejectedly at the end of the bench, barely noticing when Ben came over and patted his shoulder and told him to hang in there.

The rest of the game went by in a blur. Robbie tried to be a good teammate. He cheered loudly when a long home run by Connor put the Orioles ahead 3–2 in the fourth inning. And he shouted encouragement—shouted almost until he was hoarse—when Mike got into trouble an inning later and gave up two runs as the Rays went ahead 4–3.

But he couldn't shake the awful feeling that he'd let the whole team down—again. And when Riley struck out to end the game and the 6–3 loss was in the books, the Orioles' eleventh straight, Robbie wanted to run and hide somewhere.

As the Orioles gathered up their equipment, Willie slammed his glove against the fence.

"Second season's turning out pretty much like the first," he said.

"Only season I'm looking forward to now is the *off*-season," Carlos muttered.

"Who wants to keep playing like this?" Riley said.

"Not me," Robbie whispered as he kicked off his spikes.

And in that instant, he arrived at a decision.

He'd given it all he had. He'd tried everything to get his control back, to pitch like he used to, when he threw hard and loose and with confidence, when the ball went where he wanted it to and baseball was a joy to play.

And nothing had worked.

Dad can say whatever he wants, he thought. Same thing with Ben. But I'm not listening anymore.

Stick me in the outfield in that last game against the Yankees. Or stick me on the bench, which is probably what I deserve. I don't care.

I'm done with pitching.

Forever.

24

The Vulture was circling. Today Ms. Owens was taking the outside route around her classroom. She came within a foot of Robbie's desk on each revolution, causing his heart to flutter.

"You're roadkill, dude," Tyler Benetti whispered to Robbie. "The Vulture's gonna get you. You can see it in her eyes."

Tyler sat in the desk to Robbie's left. A short, slight kid, he had developed the ability to seemingly shrink his body mass even further and hunker down behind Robbie when the Vulture passed, which shielded him from her piercing gaze.

"Students, I hope you all enjoyed *Animal Farm* as much as I did," she said.

Robbie rolled his eyes. The Vulture looked as if she had never enjoyed anything in her life, never mind a book.

As usual, her trademark scowl was firmly in place. A tall, gaunt woman in her fifties with bony shoulders that seemed to slope inwardly, she wore a long black sweater with black polyester pants and black orthopedic shoes that made a dull, thudding sound when she walked.

It reminded Robbie of the footsteps of the dungeon master in one of his video games.

"So today," the Vulture continued, "we'll see what you've learned. Who can tell me about the theme of class stratification that runs through the book?"

Apparently, no one could. Robbie shot a quick glance at Marty, who was looking out the window, seemingly lost in another one of his fantasies.

"All right, then," the Vulture said with a tight smile as she continued circling the room. "I will have to call on our first participant."

Abruptly, she reversed direction.

What's this? Robbie thought, heart fluttering again. She never changes direction! She's coming back this way!

Now the Vulture was ten feet from Robbie's desk. She seemed to be staring right at him. He gripped the seat of his chair and steeled himself for the inevitable.

"I think we will call on . . . Mr. Benetti," Ms. Owens said at last. "Yes, you, Mr. Benetti. Almost didn't see you there. Tell us about the class stratification portrayed in this wonderful book."

Tyler turned deathly pale. Robbie smothered a laugh. On the one hand, he was sorry to see anyone caught in the Vulture's glare. On the other hand, it was pretty funny that her victim was Tyler, the kid who thought he could make himself invisible.

Plus, Robbie thought, right now it's every man for himself.

"Um . . ." Tyler began in a shaky voice. As the pause

grew longer and longer, everyone in the class had the same thought: Tyler was roadkill. The Vulture would waste no time picking his bones clean. Then they'd be bleached white by the sun.

"Class stratification . . ." Tyler repeated. He seemed frozen now, a small forlorn figure practically vibrating with fear.

The Vulture was already swooping in, making her way briskly to his desk, ready to deliver a snide remark that questioned his intelligence, ability to learn, effort with his studies, etc.

Tyler's eyes widened as she approached. Tiny beads of perspiration appeared on his forehead.

Then a familiar voice piped up.

"As everybody knows, the book demonstrates that even in societies where everyone is purportedly equal, class divisions can occur," the voice said. "Such as the one between the intelligentsia that the pigs represent and the animals that do physical labor."

It was Marty. He spoke in the slightly bored tone he always used when answering a teacher's questions, no matter what the subject.

The Vulture whirled around to face him.

"Very good, Mr. Loopus," she said. Then, narrowing her eyes and looking at the rest of the class, she added, "It's nice to see *someone* has done work for this class."

With the Vulture's back to him, Robbie pointed at Marty and silently mouthed, "Nice save."

Tyler exhaled like a convict who had just been spared the electric chair.

For the rest of the class, Robbie white-knuckled his desk each time the Vulture approached. The truth was, he had fallen behind in his reading, along with all the rest of his homework. For days he hadn't been able to concentrate on much of anything, not since his epic blowup against the Rays.

Somehow, for the next forty-five minutes, he lucked out and the Vulture didn't call on him. When the bell finally rang, he sprang from his desk and was the first one out the door. He waited for Marty in the hallway, which was now teeming with students, and the two walked to gym class together.

"Tyler owes you, big-time," Robbie said.

"So does half the school," Marty said, yawning nonchalantly. "Homework help, quiz tips, major test preparation . . ." He gestured grandly at the other kids. "I'm always there for my people."

"Modesty is your best trait," Robbie said. "Anyone ever tell you that?"

"Surprisingly, no," Marty said, grinning. "Usually they mention my superior intellect."

"Stop it," Robbie said, shaking his head. "I mean it. I'm gonna puke if I have to listen to this."

Once in the locker room, the two began changing into their gym clothes. Robbie waited until most of the other kids were outside, warming up for kickball. Then, keeping his voice low and trying to sound nonchalant, he said, "By the way, I've decided my pitching days are over."

"What?" Marty said. He stopped tying his shoes and sat bolt upright. "What are you talking about?"

"Yeah," Robbie said. "No big deal. I've had enough. Control's not getting any better. I'm still crazy wild—you saw what happened against the Rays. Anyway, I'm not pitching anymore."

"But maybe we could—" Marty said before Robbie cut him off.

"No, I've tried everything," he said, and a wave of sadness came over him, as had been happening often over the past three days. "And everyone's tried to help. Dad, you, Joey, Ben. Even Willie, Connor, and Jordy, in their own way. Now I'm just . . . done."

Marty stared at him. "Uh, have you shared this momentous decision with anyone else?" he asked finally. "Like, you know, your dad?"

Robbie nodded. "Oh yeah. Two nights ago, after dinner. Finally worked up the nerve."

"*And?*" Marty let the word hang there.

"Put it this way: he wasn't thrilled," Robbie said. "Neither was my mom. They think I'm making a big mistake."

"I'd go along with that," Marty said.

"Dad gave me that Dad Look," Robbie continued. "You know, the one where he sort of furrows his brow and looks all concerned?"

"I know that look," Marty said. "My dad gave it to me yesterday. When I got a ninety-nine instead of a hundred on the science test."

Robbie pulled on his T-shirt and sighed. "Can we make this about me instead of you? Anyway, Dad said if I quit pitching now, I'll probably regret it for the rest of my life."

"Smart man, your dad," Marty said. "Dude, you were

born to pitch! Even throwing half-speed you're faster than almost anyone else in the league! Your stuff is so good it—"

Robbie snorted. "Yeah, my stuff really dazzled the Rays," he said. "That's why they were calling me Wild Thing. How many walks did I have, forty? What good is great stuff if you can't get the ball over the plate?"

Marty shook his head sadly. From outside, they could hear the faint sounds of kids running and laughing and the soft *whoompf!* of rubber balls being kicked.

"What about Ben?" Marty said. "He's, like, your new pitching coach now, right? Did you tell him about quitting?"

"I called him yesterday," Robbie said. "He told me I was crazy. Told me not to give up. Said he was working on something that might help. Wouldn't say what. It sounded pretty mysterious."

He stood and closed his locker. "But it's too late for that," Robbie said softly. "My mind's made up. Dad's got to find someone else to pitch against the Yankees. Unless he wants Mike's arm to fall off."

They walked outside into the bright sunshine, with Marty still shaking his head. The rest of the kids were on one of the nearby fields. They heard Coach Lombardi's whistle blow as he got the class started.

"Robbie Hammond giving up pitching," Marty said. "I still can't believe you're serious."

"Serious as a heart attack, dude," Robbie said.

Then he ran to the field, toward the other kids and Coach Mike, hoping kickball would take his mind off how crappy he felt about baseball.

The Iron Mike pitching machine whirred into position and snapped forward, delivering another waist-high fastball. Robbie took a vicious cut, sending a line drive into the vast expanse of green grass in what would be right-center field if they were on an actual baseball diamond.

Ben whistled approvingly.

"That, my friend, is a *shot*!" he said. "Double all the way—even with your stubby little SpongeBob legs!"

Robbie grinned and waited for the next pitch. With no practice this afternoon—Ray Hammond had a big police departmental meeting to attend—some of the Orioles had descended on the outdoor batting cages at Grand Slam Extra, the vast baseball and softball training facility off York Road. Robbie and Marty were sharing one cage under the watchful eye of Ben, with Willie, Jordy, and Connor in the other.

As usual, Marty had wasted no time spreading the word, telling the rest of the Orioles that Robbie was through with pitching. Now the conversation centered on who else beside Mike could take the mound for the Orioles against the Yankees Saturday. The consensus seemed to be that Connor was the logical choice, since he had the strongest arm of all the position players—except Joey, who was deemed too valuable behind the plate.

"Okay, it's Connor—pending Coach's approval, of course," Ben said. "I am but a lowly assistant coach and can't make huge decisions like that."

"Coach'll go for it," Willie said confidently. "He knows Connor's a stud. With a stud arm."

"And a pea brain," Jordy said, laughing and punching Connor playfully in the shoulder.

Willie nodded. "Yes, the boy has limited intelligence," he said, keeping a straight face. "But it's the best we can do on short notice. Especially now that a certain someone has retired prematurely and left us hanging."

Robbie hung his head and said nothing.

Connor chose to ignore the jabs. "You do realize I've never pitched before, right?" he said. "Like, never ever? So I wouldn't exactly be expecting Justin Verlander out there."

"That's an all-star move, C, playing the I-never-pitched-before card," Willie said, clapping him on the back. "Way to set the bar low for yourself."

"I'm just sayin'," Connor murmured.

They were still hitting a few minutes later when a voice behind them boomed, "Well, look who's here! If it isn't the Snore-ioles."

Turning around, they saw Big Red and five other Yankees smirking and leaning against the railing. This time they wore matching Yankees workout T-shirts, and their matching Yankees gear bags were at their feet.

"We play you girls this weekend, don't we?" Big Red continued. "Last game of the season, right? Well, last game before the playoffs. Oh, wait, that's right! You guys aren't *going* to the playoffs, are you? 'Cause a team has to actually win games to go, right?"

At this, the rest of the Yankees cracked up and high-fived each other like it was the funniest thing they had ever heard.

Willie rose to the bait immediately. "Matching tees today—what a surprise," he said. "What do you do, call each other every morning to decide on the color scheme?"

Big Red's grin vanished.

But Willie wasn't through. "What're you Yankees doing here, anyway?" he said. "Shouldn't you all be getting your nails done together, too?"

Now it was the Orioles who cracked up, hooting and fist-bumping as the Yankees exchanged uneasy looks.

Big Red waited until the noise died down.

"Oh, look, there's Wild Thing!" he said, staring at Robbie. "Yeah, we heard all about your adventures against the Rays. Broke the league record for walks, didn't you? What did you have, about eighty that game?"

"Don't worry 'bout the past," Willie said. "We'll see you chumps Saturday. And wear those nice puka-shell neck-laces again. You all looked lovely in them."

Big Red started to say something. Then he spotted Marty, who was trying to hide behind the other Orioles.

"Hey, nerd!" he said, eyes narrowing. "You and I have some unfinished business, don't we?"

Marty's face drained of color.

"Only reason I'm not whipping your butt today," Big Red snarled, "is 'cause we're running late."

"Totally understand," Marty said in a high-pitched voice, holding up a trembling hand. "It's, uh, important to be on time. Promptness is a virtue. Or it should be."

Big Red scowled and took a step forward. "Are you trying to be funny?"

"Shut up! You're giving everyone a headache!"

It was Ben. Only this was Ben as Robbie and the other Orioles had never seen him. His cheeks were flushed and his eyes were angry slits. The veins in his neck were bulging.

Big Red looked Ben up and down, then turned back to Robbie.

"Wild Thing," he said with a sneer, "the quality of your bodyguards keeps going downhill. First a sixty-seven-pound nerd, now some loser with one arm. What's next, a third-grader in a wheelchair?"

Ben balled his fist and lunged at Big Red. But Robbie and Willie quickly grabbed him and held him back.

Big Red smirked and signaled to the rest of the Yankees, who seemed to bend down as one and pick up their matching gear bags.

"Okay, we're wasting time here," he said. "See you Saturday, Snore-ioles. If you even bother to show up."

By the time the Orioles finally left the batting cages a few minutes later, Ben had regained his composure. But Robbie was still fuming.

"If I didn't suck, I'd make a pitching comeback and throw some serious heat just to shut Big Red's fat mouth," he said, peeling off his batting gloves.

"Maybe it won't have to be a comeback," Ben said.

Robbie looked at him. "What do you mean?"

"Oh, nothing," Ben said. "It's just . . . you never know what can happen between now and Saturday. Maybe you'll still want to pitch."

"Trust me," Robbie said, tossing his gloves and bat in his bag. "You couldn't get me to pitch again if you held a gun to my head."

"Might not take anything that drastic," Ben said with a knowing smile.

Robbie gave him a puzzled look. But before he could say anything, Ben waved and jogged off for home.

Robbie was in a good mood when he got home from school the next day. The reality of his decision not to pitch anymore had sunk in, relieving the pressure he'd been feeling all season. And since it was a gorgeous afternoon—sunny and eighty degrees with none of the usual oppressive Baltimore humidity—he planned to meet up with Ben and Marty to shoot baskets down at the park.

But the good mood quickly evaporated when he spotted a note on the kitchen counter.

It read:

Your dad's working late, and I have a meeting with a client. Should be home by dinnertime. You're watching Ashley. Try to be nice.
    Love,
    Mom

"Watching your little sister—a fate worse than death," Robbie murmured to himself.

After he called Ben and Marty to say he couldn't make

hoops, it occurred to him that a note on the kitchen counter from one of his parents was never good news.

It never read: "Here's five dollars for ice cream—enjoy!" or "We're out buying that new skateboard you wanted! Be home soon!"

No, usually it was a note telling him to clean his room or do his homework or do something else he didn't feel like doing while they were gone—like watching his sister. That was always at the top of the don't-want-to-do list. Where was Jackie when he needed her?

Soon he heard the school bus pull up to the corner. Seconds later, Ashley came bursting through the front door.

Robbie kept his greeting short and sweet. "Mom told me to watch you. That means I'm in charge. Don't give me any trouble."

"Nice to see you too, big brother," Ashley said, throwing her backpack on the table. "Anything to eat? I'm starved."

"Then I suggest you look in the refrigerator," Robbie said. "Which is located over there."

Ashley stuck out her tongue as Robbie went down to the basement to play NBA Dunkathon, his new video game.

A few minutes later, she came down and plopped next to him on the couch.

"Uh, hello?" Robbie said. "How 'bout a little personal space?"

She smiled sweetly but didn't move. "I hear you're not pitching anymore," she said.

"News travels fast," Robbie said. "How'd you find out? They put it on the morning announcements at your school?"

Ashley shot him her pained look, the one intended to communicate what an incredible burden it was to have him for a brother.

"Mom and Dad told me. I asked them why you've been in such a crappy mood. I mean, even crappier than usual."

Robbie said nothing. Both of his hands were furiously working the controller, getting LeBron James to practically jump through the arena roof and throw down a monster jam over Kobe Bryant.

"OHHHH! IN HIS FACE!" an unseen announcer shouted. "KOBE CERTAINLY WON'T BE HAPPY AFTER THAT!"

"So why aren't you pitching?" Ashley persisted.

"Don't feel like it," Robbie said. "Know what else I don't feel like? Talking about it with you."

They sat without speaking for a moment. Robbie knew the silence wouldn't last. Ashley wasn't the type to give up easily.

"But you're such a good pitcher," she said at last.

"Ha! That's a good one!" Robbie said, eyes still glued to the screen, working LeBron into position so he could fly through the air again and dunk on poor Pau Gasol, the Lakers' big man.

Robbie tried to ignore it, but he could feel Ashley's eyes staring holes into him. Several times she seemed on the verge of saying something, then she'd catch herself.

Finally, it came out, as he knew it would.

In a soft voice, she asked, "Still scared of hitting someone?"

Robbie paused the game and put down the controller. He turned and glared at her.

"What part of 'I don't want to talk about it' don't you get?" he asked, his voice rising. "It seems so simple. Even a first grader knows what it means."

"Fine," Ashley said, standing and crossing her arms. "I know when I'm not wanted."

"This would be one of those times," Robbie agreed.

"Then play your stupid video game by yourself!" she said, stomping upstairs.

"That was the original plan," Robbie said, nodding.

A few minutes later, Robbie heard the doorbell. "Hey, Ashley! Get that, will ya?"

He was so engrossed in his game that he was surprised to look up and see Ben.

"Hope it's okay," he said. "Mom dropped me off on her way to work. Homework's all done. Instead of hanging by myself at home, I figured I'd hang with you."

"Excellent move," Robbie said, making room for him on the couch. "This is why you're coaching material."

Ben grinned. "So what's on the agenda today to improve our minds and make our parents and teachers proud of us?"

"Two words," Robbie said, pointing at the TV with his controller. "NBA Dunkathon."

"Sweet," Ben said. "The ultimate intellectual pursuit. Is there a multiplayer mode? Not that I'll be very good at using the controller. . . ."

"With your manual dexterity?" Robbie said. "You'll fig-ure out how in no time."

While Robbie set up the game, Ben went over and stud-ied the huge map of Maryland that Robbie's parents had hung on one wall.

"Ever hear of a town called Fulham?" he asked casually.

"Sure," Robbie said. "It's about forty-five minutes north-east of here. We have cousins who used to live there. Why?"

"No reason, really," Ben said. "Just there's some kid playing Babe Ruth League ball up there who sounds interesting."

"Yeah?" Robbie said distractedly.

"He's a third baseman," Ben continued. "His uniform number's ten."

Robbie turned to look at him. "*That's* what's so interesting?" he said. "A kid who plays third and wears number ten?"

"Well, no, it's not just that," Ben said. He came over to the couch, sat down, and picked up a controller.

"Oh, there's *more* to this fascinating kid?" Robbie said.

"Kind of," Ben said. "His name is Stevie Altman."

Robbie was speechless. Literally.

He tried moving his lips. They felt dry, locked in place with superglue. Nothing came out except a low, gasping sound.

Ben smiled, watching his bud's face as he struggled to get it out.

"Stevie . . . *Altman*?" Robbie finally croaked.

Ben nodded.

"*The* Stevie Altman?" Robbie said. "The one I . . ."

Ben nodded again. "Gotta be," he said. "Although he's listed as Steven Altman. Like he's all grown up or something."

Robbie stood up and paced, a dazed look on his face. "But how did you find him? I thought he was—"

"Long story," Ben said. "But I'll put it on fast-forward. I've been looking for him for a while."

"You . . . *have*?"

"Yep," Ben said. "Ever since I saw how freaked out you were throwing to me in the park that day."

Robbie looked down, embarrassed.

"It was like your head was gonna explode," Ben continued. "You were pale, sweating like a pig, your eyes were bugging out...."

"The picture of confidence—that's me," Robbie said morosely.

"Then, when you blew up against the Rays," Ben said, "I thought: Okay, this *just throw hard* stuff isn't working. We need to go in a different direction. Do something else to get him throwing the way he used to."

He stood and pointed dramatically at the map of Maryland. "Which is when I turned into—ta-daaa!—Ben Landrum: Private Investigator."

"You went up there and started poking around, looking for clues about Stevie's whereabouts?" Robbie said.

"Uh, not exactly," Ben said. "I went to my desk, sat down, and turned on the computer."

"So you were like one of those forensic scientists on TV! Combing the vast digital archives! Looking for a data trail that would lead to your man! Cyber-sleuthing!"

"Easy, dude," Ben said, putting a hand on Robbie's shoulder. "Deep breath. I just Googled him."

"Oh," Robbie said, feeling foolish.

"At first I didn't come up with anything," Ben said, sitting back down. "Because—big surprise—there are a whole lot of Steven Altmans. And there isn't a whole lot of stuff about kids on the Internet."

"You must have spent hours on this," Robbie said.

Ben grinned. "Wait till you get my bill. Your dad's going to need to take out a second mortgage. Finally I came across some lineups from a tournament in Fulham. And there it was, a Steven Altman who played for the Braves. Age twelve. Center field. Number ten in your program, number one in your hearts, as they say."

Robbie was pensive. "So he didn't move out of the state, the way everyone said."

"Apparently not," Ben said. "He moved to, quote, The Little Slice of Heaven on the Susquehanna, unquote. At least that's what they called Fulham on one of the Web sites."

"Unbelievable," Robbie said. "The other thing I can't believe is that he's still playing baseball. If you saw how hard I hit him . . . how he went down and just laid there, with that leg twitching . . ."

His voice trailed off and he shuddered.

"Well, looks like you didn't kill him, dude," Ben said. "Not only that, but the Braves play tomorrow night. I saw their schedule online. They're playing the Dodgers. Must be having a pretty good season, because it's their next-to-last game before the playoffs."

Robbie stared down at the carpet, lost in thought. "That's nice for them."

"Come on, Robbie." Ben gave him a little shove in the arm. "Let's go see him play."

"No way!" said Robbie, springing up from the couch. "I don't want to face that guy ever again. That was the worst, most embarrassing moment of my life."

"Aren't you a curious, though?" Ben asked. "You told me you're always wondering how he's doing. . . ."

"But he must hate me," Robbie said.

"Nah," said Ben, waving away the idea. "Obviously he

wasn't as traumatized as you, 'cause he's still playing. And *his* team is doing well."

Robbie winced at that irony.

"Well, *I'd* like to check him out," Ben said. "And I figured you would, too. As your coach, I think it would be good for you to see that he's okay. You don't have to talk to him if you don't want."

The idea of seeing Stevie again made Robbie's stomach churn. But he had to admit that what Ben was saying made sense. If the kid was doing well, it would put a lot to rest.

"Let's say I agree to this crazy plan," he said. "How do we get up there? Mom's got a catering gig tomorrow and—"

"All taken care of," Ben said. "I got us a great driver. Maybe you've heard of him. It's a guy by the name of Coach Ray Hammond."

The ride to Fulham the next afternoon seemed
to take forever.

Interstate 95 was backed up for miles with rush-hour traffic, and it took close to an hour just to reach the Perryville toll plaza. Robbie sat up front with his dad, and Ben and Marty were in the backseat.

At lunch Robbie had told Marty everything: about beaning Stevie Altman, about how it had weighed on him all these months and sent him into a panic whenever he took the mound, and about how Ben had tracked Stevie down on the Internet.

Marty had listened wide-eyed to the whole story, without interrupting once. After that, he had promptly insisted on coming along to Fulham to provide, as he put it, "intellectual processing" of what they might see.

Now, as they drove along the Susquehanna River, flanked by tall evergreen trees jutting up into the clear blue sky, Marty was regaling the car's occupants with trivia in what the other kids called his "Professor Marty" voice.

"The Mighty Susquehanna," he said. "That's what

they call it. Did you know that with its watershed it's the sixteenth-largest river in the United States?"

Ben stared at him and slowly shook his head. "No, Marty," he said. "No one in the whole freakin' world knows that. Or cares. Except you."

Marty seemed pleased to hear that. "Well, it's true," he said. "And it's the longest river in the country that's non-navigable for commercial boat traffic."

"Let me ask you a question," Ben said. "Why are you so fascinated by useless information like that?"

Marty was incredulous. *"Useless?"* he said. "What if you were, like, the captain of an oil tanker, okay? And you want to know: can I bring my tanker safely down the Susquehanna? Wouldn't be useless information then, would it?"

He smiled and crossed his arms, looking satisfied with himself again.

"But you're *not* the captain of a tanker," Ben said. "You're in seventh grade. You don't even ride a bike. So why do you care if the Susquehanna River is non- . . . non—whatever that word is—to commercial boat traffic?"

"Non-navigable," Marty said. "It means—"

"I *know* what it means," Ben said, an edge to his voice. "But why do you *care* that the river is non-navigable?"

Marty threw up his hands and sighed. "I don't know why I bother," he said. "I try to enlighten you guys. Try to talk about interesting things that—"

"That's not interesting," Ben interrupted. "The fact that the Susquehanna is the sixteenth-largest river in the U.S. is not interesting. In the least. Now, if you told us the

Susquehanna was the only river in the country filled with flesh-eating piranha, *that* would be interesting."

Marty looked at him as if he'd lost his mind.

"Or," Ben continued, "if you said that vampires lived along the Susquehanna and they come out at night to suck the blood out of innocent citizens, *that* would be interesting. But that other stuff isn't interesting."

"Whatever," Marty said. He made a big show of turning away from Ben and looking out the window. "I have some cool facts about the Susquehanna watershed, too. But now I'll keep them to myself. Your loss."

Listening to all this in the front, Robbie and his dad looked at each other and chuckled.

Normally, Robbie enjoyed hearing Marty discourse about something that excited him. His chatter had become soothing background music for Robbie. It helped him relax, assured him that Marty was on top of things and all was right with the world.

But today Robbie was preoccupied with other thoughts, all of them having to do with Stevie Altman.

What would they find out when they finally saw Stevie play?

Would he still be the same great, fearless player he was before a wild pitch crashed into his skull?

Or was he just a shell of his old self now, a kid who trembled with fear each time he stepped into the batter's box, the way Robbie did when a hitter stepped in against him?

And what if it wasn't the right Stevie Altman? What if they had driven all this way only to watch some stranger? For all they knew, the Stevie Altman they were looking for could live thousands of miles away. Robbie might be destined to spend the rest of his life wondering whatever happened to the kid he beaned in an all-star game on a long-ago summer night.

Twenty minutes later, they turned off the highway and onto a dirt road marked by a sign that read: LANDIS FIELD— A LITTLE SLICE OF BASEBALL HEAVEN.

"Boy, they're big on little slices of heaven, aren't they?" Ben said.

As soon as they stopped, Robbie jumped from the car and ran to the bleachers. He clambered to the top to get a good view of the entire field.

His dad and friends joined him as the Braves were coming to bat. The scoreboard said it was the bottom of the third inning, 3–1 Braves. Robbie craned his neck to get a look at the Braves dugout, but the sun reflecting off the protective screen in front made it impossible to see inside.

"Top of the order—let's go, Braves!" shouted a dad sitting in front of them. Robbie scanned the crowd for Stevie's parents, but they were nowhere in sight.

Now the Braves leadoff hitter strolled to the plate and another kid moved into the on-deck circle, swinging a weighted bat in lazy circles.

Robbie drummed his fingers nervously on the metal railing. "Where *is* he?" he said, louder than he'd intended.

"Easy, son," Ray Hammond said, draping an arm around Robbie's shoulders. "If he's here, we'll see him soon enough."

"Wouldn't it be funny if he, like, had the flu?" Marty said. "And he's home in bed?"

The others stared at Marty, who looked over and said, "What?"

"That would be *funny* to you?" Ben said. "The kid getting sick? After we drove, like, nine hundred hours to get here?"

"Okay, maybe not ha-ha funny," Marty said. "Maybe funny, like, weird."

"Uh, no," Ben said. "How about we just watch the game? And one of us—not saying who—stops talking?"

"Fine," Marty mumbled. He slouched down and lapsed into a sulky silence.

The Braves leadoff hitter drew a walk from the Dodgers pitcher, a lanky right-hander with a decent fastball, and another Brave popped out of the dugout and headed for the on-deck circle.

Still no sign of Stevie. Robbie watched with mounting anxiety as the Braves' number two hitter singled to right field, the runner on first wheeling around second base and sliding into third ahead of the throw.

This time no one came out to the on-deck circle as the next Braves batter stepped in. After working the count to 2–2, the kid hit a sharp comebacker to the mound. The Dodgers pitcher handled it easily, checking the runner at third before throwing to first for the out.

Now there was a lull in the game.

A full thirty seconds went by and still no new batter appeared. The home plate umpire took off his mask and stared into the Braves dugout. Finally a figure appeared on the top step, his back to the field. He gestured to someone on the bench, as if he'd forgotten something, like maybe his batting gloves.

When he turned, Robbie could see it was a tall, thickly built boy holding a bat in one hand and a batting helmet in the other. He rested the bat between his legs, flicked his long, dark hair back, and jammed the helmet on his head. He took a languid practice swing and walked unhurriedly to the plate, bouncing lightly on the balls of his feet.

"It's him!" Robbie said, his heart pounding.

"Cha-ching!" Ben said in a hushed voice. "So, he's their money hitter! Now batting cleanup, number ten . . . Stevie Altman!"

He was taller than the last time Robbie had seen him, and stronger-looking too. His chest seemed to strain against his jersey, as if when the Braves handed out uniforms, he got stuck with a medium instead of a large. But there was no mistaking that it was Stevie. The kid exuded the same quiet confidence as before.

He took his time getting settled in the batter's box, digging in with his right foot and then planting his left foot only when he was ready. Gently, he tapped the outside corner of the plate with his bat, making sure he could reach a pitch out there if he had to.

Then he seemed to nod almost imperceptibly at the pitcher—*Okay, I'm ready*—and he stood there with the bat held high, waiting patiently for whatever the kid wanted to throw.

Watching this, Robbie felt a wave of relief go through him.

"That's what I remember," he whispered to the others. "Look how relaxed he is up there!"

"Any more relaxed, he'd be asleep," Ben muttered.

The Dodgers pitcher started him off with a fastball that was just outside. But Stevie didn't swing. Instead, he seemed to watch it all the way into the catcher's glove. Then he stepped out and nonchalantly blew a huge bubble while taking a practice swing.

"He did that to me, too," Robbie whispered. "Like he was studying my fastball under a microscope. And he wasn't that impressed."

"No wonder you wanted to whiff him," Marty said. "Gives you no respect. If I was a pitcher, I'd be ticked."

"If you were a pitcher," Ben said, nudging Robbie, "it would set baseball back two hundred years."

"Ha-ha, very funny," Marty said as the two other boys smothered giggles.

Now the Dodgers pitcher went after Stevie with a hard, nasty curveball that seemed to break somewhere out by the Braves dugout.

Robbie could tell right away that Stevie was anything but gun-shy. He stood in there all the way until the pitch dipped near his left shoulder and just missed inside for ball two.

Then it was the same ritual: step out, casually blow a bubble, take another little practice swing.

"Wow! That was one sick breaking ball!" Ben said.

"Stevie's measuring the pitcher, all right," Robbie's dad said in a low voice. "Wants to see what the kid has. And he's only gonna swing if it's a strike."

He turned to look at the three boys. "Now tell me again, class," he said. "What do you call it when the pitcher's two-and-oh on the batter?"

"Hitter's count!" they said in unison. "Look for a pitch you can drive!"

Ray Hammond grinned. "Very good, students. Now we'll see what happens next."

What happened next, they would all agree later, was a big-time mistake by the Dodgers pitcher.

Worried about walking Stevie, he tried to slip a belt-high fastball past him. Stevie's bat was a blur. He took a short, compact swing—the textbook swing every baseball coach in the world wants his players to take.

They heard the muffled *ping-g-g!* of the bat, and the ball rocketed into the gap in left-center as the fielders gave chase and two runs scored.

"Smoked!" Ben said as the Braves' parents leaped to their feet and cheered. "The kid's got a little thunder in his bat, doesn't he?"

Stevie cruised into second base, calmly blowing another bubble as the Braves dugout erupted with chants of "STEE-VEE! STEE-VEE!"

"You know something?" Marty said. "I'm starting to hate that kid. And I don't even know him. He makes it look so easy."

Robbie nodded. He couldn't take his eyes off Stevie, who wasn't even breathing hard as he coolly peeled off his batting gloves and stuck them in his back pocket.

Ben clapped Robbie on the back. "Dude?" he said. "Can we all agree on something? That whatever you did in that all-star game did not exactly bring the kid's baseball career to a crashing halt?"

Robbie simply nodded again. He was afraid to look over

at Ben, afraid his bud would see the tears of happiness he was blinking back.

For the rest of the game, Robbie couldn't stop smiling as his eyes followed Stevie everywhere.

The big kid played center field for the Braves and had only one ball hit his way, a shot in the right-center gap that he cut off nicely, holding the batter to a long single. But he came to bat two more times, hitting a long fly ball to left in the fifth inning, and then driving in another run with a double in the sixth as the Braves broke the game wide open with four more runs.

It was getting dark when the game ended, with the final score Braves 10, Dodgers 2. As the two teams lined up to shake hands, Robbie's dad leaned over and asked, "Want to go say hi to Stevie? See how he's doing?"

Robbie thought about it for a moment.

"No, that's okay, Dad," he said. "I can see how he's doing. He's doing just fine."

Then his smile widened even more. "Besides," he added, "we gotta get ready to play the Yankees. Remember that pain-in-the-neck kid on your team who said he didn't want to pitch anymore? Well, he's definitely changed his mind."

Now Ray Hammond was smiling too. So were Ben and Marty.

"Coach," Ben said, jerking his head in the direction of the parking lot, "let's go home. Looks like our work here is done."

It was Friday evening and the Orioles were gathered in a side room at Gino's Burger Barn, consuming food at an astonishing rate.

Burgers piled high with pickles, onions, lettuce, and tomato were being inhaled. Orders of fries seemed to disappear the moment they were set down. Enough pitchers of soda had been consumed to suggest that the team had just returned from a ten-mile hike through Death Valley.

The shaken waitstaff had never seen anything like it. These twelve-year-olds were scarfing down food and drink as if they were the Baltimore Ravens.

"I'm afraid to put my hand on the table—they'll devour that, too," one server said.

"Probably not the *whole* hand," Ray Hammond said with a chuckle. "Maybe just a couple of fingers."

"I can't afford to lose any of those," Ben said. "That's why I'm sitting here with Coach."

The impromptu team meeting had been Robbie's idea. A thought had been gnawing at him ever since the long drive back from Fulham.

In less than twenty-four hours, the Orioles would take the field against Big Red and the Yankees in the final game of the season. Before they did, Robbie had decided, there was a bit of business he needed to take care of.

He was nervous as he pushed away from the table, almost as nervous as he'd been facing hitters all season. He took a deep breath and nodded at Ben, who banged the table with a fork, signaling for quiet. Robbie stood and looked around at the faces of his teammates, all of them staring at him with puzzled looks.

"Ahem," he said, clearing his throat.

"Good start, dude," Willie said. "Glad we got our parents to drive us here for that."

The rest of the Orioles chuckled.

"But at least the burgers are good," Joey said. "And Coach is paying for them, too!"

This triggered a fresh wave of laughter, along with a chant of: "COACH! COACH! COACH!"

Coach grinned and held up his hands. "I'll pay," he said, "but only if you listen to Robbie first. That's the deal."

When the table had quieted down, Robbie tried again. "First, I . . . I want to apologize to you guys," he began.

For the next ten minutes, he told them all about the incident that had haunted him for the past year.

He told them about the awful June day when he had hit Stevie Altman, about how much it had shaken him, about how he'd had a knot in his stomach and trembled with fear every time he'd taken the mound since, certain he would put another kid in the hospital and mess him up for life.

Then he told them about his going to Fulham to watch Stevie play, about finding the kid looking as strong and confident at the plate as ever, and about how this had lifted a huge weight from Robbie's shoulders.

When he was through, a hush fell over the room.

Finally Willie said: "Dude, why didn't you tell us you were freaked out about hitting a kid?"

"Yeah," Jordy said. "We thought you just, you know, sucked."

Now the entire table dissolved in laughter again, with Robbie laughing the hardest. Then he grew serious again.

"It was a mistake not to tell you guys," he said softly. "I almost told you that night at the carnival. And then at lunch that Monday."

"Then why *didn't* you?" Connor pressed.

"Lots of reasons," Robbie said. "I was embarrassed, for one thing. I thought you'd think I was a wuss. Like: 'Okay, you hit a kid, big deal. Now get over it.'"

He looked over at his dad, who nodded encouragingly.

"The other thing was, I thought I could get over it by myself," Robbie continued. "I thought if I just gave it time and tried a few things, I'd forget about Stevie. And get my control back."

He shook his head sadly. "But that sure didn't work. I'm just glad Ben realized it wasn't *going* to work, either."

All eyes turned to Ben, who gave Robbie the thumbs-up sign.

"Anyway," Robbie said, "I'm sorry I kept the secret from you. Sorry I killed our season, too."

He looked down as the rest of the Orioles exchanged uneasy glances.

"You didn't kill our season, dude," Joey said. "We *all* killed our season. After all, no one else except Mike could pitch anyway. And we didn't hit a lick all year long. Plus our fielding was awful."

"Other than that," Mike said, "we had a pretty good team."

They all chuckled ruefully.

"But here's the good news," Robbie continued. "I'm not afraid to pitch anymore. Might be hard to believe, but it's true. And we've got one more game left, right? Against the Yankees. And I really, really want to beat those guys."

"Yeah," Connor said. "Wouldn't it be great to stick it to Big Red?"

"And the rest of the Yankee Barbies," Willie said, to more chuckles. "With their matching spring ensembles."

"Yeah, but who are we kidding?" Jordy said now. "We can't beat those guys. They're the best team in the league. And Big Red's an absolute beast who kicked our butts last time."

A gloomy silence descended on the room again.

Suddenly Marty shot a hand in the air.

"Again with the hand!" Willie said, shaking his head. "Like it's science class."

"Oooh, oooh!" Marty cried. "Can I say something?"

"If we said no," Jordy said, "would it matter?"

With that, Marty leaped to his feet and began pacing the room. "Why *can't* we beat the Yankees?" he said. "Since time immemorial, there have been underdogs who defied the odds."

"Time immemorial," Willie repeated, rolling his eyes.

"Here we go," Gabe muttered. "It's showtime. Marty's all wound up from the soda."

"The three hundred Spartans," Marty continued, his voice rising. "Weren't they underdogs? Three hundred soldiers against the entire Persian army at Thermopylae?"

"Yeah, and they all got slaughtered," Connor said. "I saw the movie."

"But they lasted for seven days!" Marty said. "Held off three hundred thousand Persians. Totally beat the odds."

"How did they beat the odds," Connor asked, "when they all ended up with, like, spears through their chests?"

"And arrows through their throats," Gabe said.

"And swords through their hearts," Mike said.

Marty ignored them, pacing even more briskly now.

"And what about David versus Goliath?" he went on. "Little David with his humble sling against big ol' Goliath with his sword and armor and whatnot. What about Cinderella? And Harry Potter?"

"I don't know," Gabe said. "Harry Potter could kick some serious butt when he had to, bro."

"SO CAN WE!" Marty thundered. He walked up behind Robbie and put a hand on his shoulder. "And here's the guy who will lead us. My man Robert William Hammond is back, dudes!"

All eyes turned to Robbie, who sat there thinking, Please don't start with that legend stuff again.

"Yes," Marty said, his voice dropping to a dramatic hush.

"He'll pitch his heart out for us tomorrow. And the rest of us will come up big, too. We'll hit against the Yankees. We'll field against the Yankees. We'll be aggressive on the bases against the Yankees. I can feel it. And ultimately, we'll beat them. First win of the season coming up, dudes."

"Poof!" Joey said, pretending to wave a magic wand. "Just like that?"

"Just like that," Marty said. "Remember: what the mind believes, the body can achieve."

"I like that one," Willie said, grinning. "Whose quote is that?"

"I forget, but that's not important," Marty said. He pointed a bony finger at his teammates. "What's important is that we go out there tomorrow thinking we can beat the Yankees. Let's play out of our minds, dudes. What've we got to lose?"

He sat down with a self-satisfied smile. Then he looked over at Robbie's dad.

"Coach," he said, "any more burgers coming out?"

Thick, dark clouds hung low in the sky as the Orioles and Yankees warmed up a half hour before game time the next day. Out beyond the right-field fence was what everyone was calling Camp Yankees, a jumble of Yankees folding chairs and Yankees tents manned by the players' parents, who were outfitted in enough Yankees foul-weather gear to withstand a Category 5 hurricane.

Just as the Orioles prepared to take the infield, a fog-horn voice cut through the air: "HEY, SNORE-IOLES! GET READY FOR A MAJOR BEATDOWN!"

"Gee, I wonder who that could be?" Willie said, not bothering to look.

"Could it be the human hairball himself, Big Red?" Connor said.

"WE'RE GONNA SMACK YOU LIKE A PIÑATA, SNORE-IOLES!" the voice cried.

"Puh-leeze," Willie said, rolling his eyes. "Come up with better material, son."

But none of the Orioles said anything back. At the Burger Barn the night before, right after Marty's Three Hundred

Spartans speech, they had made a pact: no trash-talking today. Take care of business. Focus on the game.

Get their first—okay, *only*—win of the season.

And do it with class.

This was Coach's idea. Ben's, too.

"Keep your eyes on the prize," Coach had told them. "All that other stuff, the yapping at the other team and whatnot, saps your concentration."

"Also drains your energy levels," Ben had said. "I read a story about an NBA player who said he'd be gassed by the end of the first quarter if he was talking mad trash. He decided he'd play harder if he just shut up."

So as Big Red continued to taunt the Orioles, Willie simply smiled at him and waved pleasantly, muttering under his breath, "What a first-class dork."

One by one, the rest of the Orioles smiled and waved too.

"Jerk," Connor whispered.

"Dork," Gabe hissed.

"Loser," Marty murmured.

The sight of all this smiling and waving seemed to puzzle Big Red. He glared at them for a moment. Then he turned and walked slowly back to the Yankees dugout, shaking his head.

The Orioles smothered their laughter.

"The boy has no clue!" Marty said.

"Probably pretty much how he goes through life," Willie said.

When the Orioles took the field to start the game, Robbie sprinted to the mound. He looked up at the threatening sky and said a silent prayer. *Please, no rainout. Not today. Not against these guys.*

He had never felt more ready to pitch a game in his life. Warming up, he threw effortlessly, hitting whatever target Joey gave him, the ball popping into the big catcher's mitt with a loud, satisfying *WHAP!*

Last night, Robbie had been so psyched to face the Yankees that he had tossed and turned in bed for hours. Today he was raring to go. So were the rest of the Orioles. He could read it in their faces. *Last game, nothing to lose, let's do this.*

"Throwing strikes now!" his dad yelled. "Just like the old days!"

When the Yankees leadoff hitter stepped in against him, Robbie couldn't wipe the smile off his face. He wasn't trying to show the kid up. He was just amazed at how relaxed and confident he felt.

Joey put down one finger. Fastball. Robbie nodded and went into his windup. Today, he thought, you'll taste the *real* Robbie Hammond heater.

The batter never had a chance.

The ball was on him before he could react. It was belt-high and tantalizing—if you could actually see it. But the kid was just moving the bat off his shoulder—probably thinking: *Uh-oh, here it is, do I swing?*—when the ball slammed into Joey's glove for strike one.

The next two pitches were similar. Robbie reared back and fired, and the batter flailed away at two straight blistering fastballs. He was already walking back to the dugout, shaking his head as Joey whipped the ball down to Carlos at third.

"Whoa!" said a voice behind Robbie. He turned to see Willie staring at him in astonishment.

"Robert William Hammond," Willie said, "that is some *serious* cheese you're throwing!"

Robbie nodded and tugged the brim of his cap down low. This was his all-business look. You don't need a game face, he thought, when you're throwing serious—what did Willie call it?—*cheese*. But a game face doesn't hurt, either.

The next batter went down on four pitches, managing to foul off the second before Robbie finished him off with two letter-high fastballs. Now he could hear a buzz coming from the Yankees dugout. *Who is this kid?* was the gist of the murmured conversation. The Yankees were seeing a completely different pitcher than the timid, erratic soul they'd seen last time. And they didn't seem thrilled.

The Orioles, on the other hand, seemed totally energized by their pitcher's performance. When Robbie got the next batter on a weak dribbler to the mound to retire the side, the Orioles sprinted off the field, hooting and slapping gloves, more excited than Robbie had seen them all season. He looked over at his dad, who gave him a big smile and a thumbs-up as he headed out to coach third base.

"Keep pounding that fastball," Ben said. "Throw as hard as you can for as long as you can. If you get tired, we'll bring in Mike."

"Yeah," Marty added. "Remember what Plato said: 'Better a little which is well done, than a great deal imperfectly.'"

Ben shot him a look. "Unless Plato was a pitching coach," he said dryly, "we probably don't need to be quoting him right at this moment."

"Whatever," Marty said, sulking. "That's what I get for trying to help people."

The Orioles' sense of elation didn't last long. Big Red was on the mound for the Yankees, and he was throwing almost as hard as Robbie. Willie drew a leadoff walk on a 3–2 count, but Big Red settled down after that to strike out Joey and Jordy and get Connor on a foul pop to the third baseman.

Robbie was about to take the mound again when Joey shuffled over, his shin guards flapping.

"You know who leads off for them this inning, right?"

Robbie grinned. "Lemme guess," he said. "Big kid? Red hair? Big muscles?"

Joey grunted. "Fits the general description. 'Cept you forgot to add big mouth."

"My bad," Robbie said. "Think we can close that yap for him?"

The catcher looked at him, a smile forming at the corners of his mouth. "You know," he said as the two bumped fists, "I believe we can."

As Robbie warmed up, Big Red glared at him from the on-deck circle before swaggering to the plate. Robbie had to give him credit: the kid didn't lack for confidence. The rest of the Yankees already seemed intimidated about facing Robbie and his heater. But not Big Red. As he dug in, he wore the same smirk he'd had that day at the batting cages, the same smirk he'd worn the last time the two teams met.

"PITCHER'S GOT NUTHIN', HONEY!" a shrill female voice yelled from the stands. "TOTAL RAG ARM! TAKE HIM DEEP! JUST LIKE LAST TIME!"

Ah, Robbie thought, that must be Big Red's mom. *Sounds as pleasant as her kid.* For an instant, he wondered where Big Red's dad was. Probably back home, yelling at little kids to stay off his lawn.

Robbie was amped. Since seeing Stevie Altman, all he had thought about was Big Red and striking him out. But maybe he was a little too amped now. He rocked, kicked, and fired a chin-high fastball that Joey had to leap to corral.

Ball one.

Big Red stepped out and sneered. "Wild thing," he sang, "you make my heart sing. . . ."

"Knock it off, batter," the ump barked.

"Sure, Mr. Umpire," Big Red said sarcastically. "You're totally the boss."

Robbie was livid. He could feel his heart thumping in his chest. He took a deep breath and remembered Ben's advice: *Don't overthrow.* This is what you've been waiting for, he told himself. Don't blow it. Go get the big jerk.

Just like that, he felt an eerie calm come over him again. His next pitch was a laser on the outside corner. Big Red swung from his heels. His bat caught nothing but air.

Strike one.

Joey put down one finger again. Robbie nodded, went

into his windup, and fired. Fastball, inside. Big Red swung even harder this time, grunting from the effort. The muscles in his forearms seemed to ripple. But the ball popped harmlessly into Joey's glove.

Strike two.

Behind him, Robbie could hear the Orioles pounding their gloves and yelling encouragement, their cheers getting louder with each pitch.

Big Red stepped out. Now the smirk was gone, replaced by a look of . . . well, Robbie wasn't sure. Confusion? Uncertainty? Shaking his head and muttering to himself, Big Red seemed to take forever before he stepped back in.

"THAT'S OKAY, YOU STILL GOT HIM, HONEY!" the voice from the stands yelled. "SHOW THAT LITTLE LOSER WHAT YOU GOT!"

This time Robbie made Big Red wait. He stared in at the big guy for what seemed like ten seconds. Finally he reared back and fired, a high fastball that seemed to dart and rise on its way to the plate.

Big Red swung so hard he fell down, ending up sprawled in the dirt as players from both teams giggled uncontrollably.

"Strike three!" the ump cried.

Which is when Big Red had a meltdown.

First he swung the bat high over his head and brought it crashing down on the plate. Then he yanked off his batting helmet and fired it into the Yankees dugout, scattering a few teammates.

In a flash, the umpire whipped off his mask. Robbie could see it was the same ump who had worked the first

Orioles-Yankees game, the same ump Big Red had jawed at after homering off Robbie.

His face contorted with anger, the ump started to raise his right hand, his thumb jutting upward.

Which was when Robbie said another silent prayer.

No, please don't toss him, ump! I want to do that again.

A figure popped out of the Yankees dugout and sprinted to the plate. It was their coach. Before the ticked-off umpire could react, the coach grabbed Big Red by the shoulders and hustled him off the field, murmuring apologetically, "Heh-heh, no need for any ejections, ump. The boy just got a little excited. He's very sorry for his behavior, aren't you, son?"

"Not really," Big Red snarled, squirming to escape the coach's grasp.

Now a woman dressed in a Yankees satin jacket and skinny jeans, with flaming red hair piled high on her head, tottered onto the field in high heels.

"STOP MANHANDLING MY SON, YOU BIG OX!" she screeched, advancing on the startled Yankees coach.

"Mom, you're embarrassing me!" Big Red shouted, a look of alarm on his face.

As the umpire and the two coaches attempted to calm the irate woman and restore order, Robbie and Joey huddled with the Orioles infielders near the mound. They held their gloves to their faces so no one could see them laughing.

"Win or lose," Willie said, "this is the greatest game ever!"

"Yeah, well guess what? We ain't losing," Joey growled.

"You're right," Willie said. "Let's win this sucker. Assuming the game ever continues, that is."

They looked over near the Yankees dugout, where Big Red's mom was still carrying on, her decibel level nearing that of a chain saw roaring to life.

"No wonder Big Red's got so many, um, *issues*," Willie said, shaking his head.

Now Ben walked out to join them.

"Guys," he said, "don't let Big Red and his crazy mom distract you. Stay loose. Throw the ball around. Focus on the game. None of this other stuff matters."

The Orioles nodded. They broke up the mound conference and played catch to keep their arms warm. Still, it took another five minutes for Big Red's enraged mom to be coaxed off the field. And this happened only after the ump waved his cell phone in front of her like it was pepper spray and threatened to call the police and forfeit the game to the Orioles if she didn't leave immediately.

"YOU WOULDN'T DARE!" Big Red's mom shouted.

"Try me," the ump said calmly. "And by the way? You are to leave the premises altogether."

When he began dialing 9-1-1 with one beefy finger, Big Red's mom stamped her high heels in frustration and stalked out to the parking lot.

When the game finally resumed, the low rumble of

thunder could be heard off in the distance. Robbie looked up anxiously. The storm was getting closer. He found himself working even more quickly now, striking out the next batter on four pitches before getting the Yankees number six hitter to ground out to Jordy to end the inning.

"Need some runs!" Ben said as the Orioles hustled off the field, high-fiving Robbie. "Can't win if we don't score."

But from there, the game settled into a classic pitchers' duel. The two teams were still locked in a scoreless tie in the bottom of the fourth inning. Big Red was just as dominating on the mound as Robbie was—by league rules, both boys could pitch the full six innings, since neither team had played another game that week.

In the Orioles dugout, the tension was increasing. Here they were, so close to their only win of the season, finally getting a dominating performance from their own pitcher—yet they seemed as helpless at the plate against Big Red as the Yankees were against Robbie.

As Big Red warmed up to start the fourth, the Orioles saw Ben walk up to Coach in the dugout and whisper in his ear. Coach nodded and said, "Good idea." He clapped his hands and gathered the Orioles around him.

"I think we can agree Big Red's pitching a heck of a game," he began.

"Gee, what makes you say that, Coach?" Marty said. "Just 'cause the kid's got, like, eight strikeouts? And looks like Tim Lincecum out there?"

Coach ignored the sarcasm. "So we're playing 'small ball' this inning," he continued. "Which means everyone's up there bunting. Let's see if Big Red can field as well as he pitches. See how good the catcher and corner infielders are, too."

The Orioles looked at each other and shrugged. Why not? Nothing else was working.

Joey led off and pushed a bunt down the first base line that he beat out when Big Red was slow getting off the mound. Jordy sacrificed the runner to second with another bunt right back to the pitcher. Then Connor's bunt in front of the plate was pounced on by the Yankees catcher, who made a nice throw to first for the second out.

But now Joey was at third. The Orioles' first run was a mere sixty feet away. And the Yankees seemed shaken by what was happening.

When Carlos popped up yet another bunt attempt, the third baseman was so rattled that he stumbled, breaking in on the ball, and dropped it. And there was Carlos, safe at first as Joey crossed the plate with the game's first run.

Big Red stared daggers at the third baseman, who hung his head and kicked at the dirt.

"Be nice if *someone* could catch the freakin' ball!" the pitcher said loudly. He grabbed the rosin bag and slammed it down in disgust as the Yankees infielders glanced at each other and shook their heads.

The next batter, Riley, also popped up his bunt attempt, but this time it was gloved by the catcher for the third out. Still, the Orioles' strategy had worked to perfection.

Orioles 1, Yankees 0.

If they could hang on for two more innings . . .

As Robbie warmed up, the sky looked even more ominous. But he knew that if the weather held up, the game was far from over. He had seen too many other teams get overconfident and blow the lead with careless play. And how many times had he watched a pitcher ease up in the late innings and get hammered?

No way I'm easing up, he thought. Not now. Not with a chance to finally get a win for these guys after the crappy season I helped put them through.

He struck out the first Yankees batter on three straight letter-high fastballs. The next kid was clearly trying to draw a walk, crouching so low it was comical. But Robbie didn't care how small the strike zone was now—he didn't care if it was the size of a party napkin. He blew three straight fastballs by that kid, too.

Two outs. The thunder was getting louder now. It was getting darker. The air smelled thick with rain.

And coming to bat for the Yankees was none other than Big Red.

"TIME!" a voice cried, and Ben bounded out of the Orioles dugout.

When he reached the mound, he said, "Coach sent me out here. Says he's too nervous to come out and talk to you himself."

Robbie nodded. "Dad gets like that sometimes."

Ben looked in at the plate, where Big Red was scowling and taking vicious practice cuts, his big black bat whistling through the air.

"You knew it would come down to this, right?" Ben said. "You against him? Probably for the game?"

Robbie grinned. "Actually, I didn't," he said. "But I kinda hoped it would."

"Don't get cocky," Ben warned. "Be careful with him. The kid's a tool, sure. But he's a dangerous hitter, too. One swing and the game could be tied."

Robbie nodded. "I have a plan," he said quietly.

Ben studied him. "A plan, huh?" he said. "Any chance of sharing it with the rest of your team?"

"No, I don't think so," Robbie said. "That way if it doesn't work, it's all on me."

Ben rolled his eyes and turned to go. "Great," he said. "That ought to *really* make your dad feel better."

Actually, Robbie *did* have a plan. It was something he'd been thinking about since he struck out Big Red in the second inning, a plan for how to pitch the big slugger so he didn't get lucky and catch up to a fastball and launch it into lunar orbit like last game.

As Big Red dug in, Robbie peered in for the sign. Joey put down one finger. Robbie shook him off.

He could almost hear his catcher thinking: *Whaa? What are you doing?*

Joey put down one finger again, more emphatically this time.

Again, Robbie shook him off. He could see Joey's puzzled look behind the thick face mask, but this was no time for explanations.

Finally, Joey shrugged and put down two fingers.

Curveball.

Robbie nodded.

Perfect.

Just as he'd expected, Big Red was waiting on the fastball, all keyed up to get the bat started early after his humiliating strikeout in the second inning. The big, slow curve took him completely by surprise. He stood frozen, the bat still on his shoulder, while the ball dipped over the plate at the last minute for strike one.

Now a lightbulb seemed to switch on in Joey's brain, just like in the cartoons.

Ohhh, I get it.

He put down two fingers again. Robbie nodded and went into his windup. This time the ball seemed headed straight for Big Red's left shoulder. But just as he leaped back to avoid it, it broke sharply across the plate for strike two.

"HOO-EE!" Joey cried, firing the ball back to Robbie. "That's one sick hook!"

Big Red stepped out, muttering to himself. Robbie felt a raindrop hit his arm. Then he felt a few more, and a few more after that. He looked up at the sky, almost black now. It was going to pour any minute.

This time, he didn't wait for a sign. As soon as Big Red stepped back in, Robbie went into his windup. He kicked, rocked, and delivered, snapping his wrist hard. The ball was on its way, spinning mesmerizingly toward the plate.

Only . . . Big Red was ready for a breaking ball this time. But not *this* breaking ball. As he swung, the ball seemed to swerve and drop straight down, landing in Joey's mitt with a soft *WHUMP*!

Strike three.

"NO-O-O!" Big Red screamed, tomahawking the plate with his bat again. Now lightning streaked across the sky and the loud crack of thunder made them all jump. The rain started gushing in thick, gray sheets.

The ump whipped off his mask and waved his hands high in the air.

Ball game over.

Final score: Orioles 1, Yankees 0.

The rest of the Orioles came sprinting toward Robbie, ignoring the downpour. Marty was the first to reach him, whooping and jumping on his back. Robbie saw his dad and Ben coming toward him, too.

"Never been prouder of you, son!" Coach said.

"Do you even remember what a win feels like?" Ben yelled, draping his arm around Robbie's neck as they all ran for cover.

Robbie beamed, the raindrops bouncing off his face like tiny clear pebbles.

"Tell you the truth," he said, "I almost forgot."

It was a lazy Monday afternoon, and Robbie, Marty, and Ben were back at Eddie Murray Field. The big thunderstorm of two days ago had left everything looking fresh and green and shiny. The cinnamon-colored base paths had been raked smooth, and the smell of new-mown grass filled the air.

The end of baseball season always made Robbie sad. But there was no place on earth he'd rather be today, throwing the ball around with his buds.

They were playing their favorite game again: diving over the rickety outfield fence to rob imaginary home run balls, each boy taking a turn with the play-by-play call:

"THERE'S A DRIVE TO DEEP CENTER FIELD . . . THIS ONE HAS A CHANCE . . . BUT, WAIT, HERE COMES LOOPUS! LOOK AT HIM RUN ON THOSE SPINDLY LEGS! NOW HE NEARS THE WALL AND ELEVATES . . . AND SOMEHOW HE COMES DOWN WITH THE BALL!"

"THAT BALL IS CRUSHED! LANDRUM GIVING CHASE . . . HE LEAPS AND . . . LADIES AND GENTLEMEN, I'VE NEVER SEEN ANYTHING LIKE IT! BEN LANDRUM, THE

ONE-ARMED PHENOM YOU'VE HEARD SO MUCH ABOUT, JUST MADE A CATCH FOR THE AGES!"

"TWO–TWO COUNT . . . DON'T WANT TO MAKE A MISTAKE HERE . . . OH, HE HIT THAT A TON! HAMMOND GOES BACK . . . STILL GOING BACK . . . AT THE WARNING TRACK, AT THE WALL . . . NOW HE DIVES TOWARD THE SEATS AND . . . YES-S-S! SOMEHOW HE MAKES THE GRAB!"

A half hour later, sweaty and tired, they sprawled in the grass behind second base. The conversation quickly turned to Saturday's game and the exciting finish.

"Big Red went majorly psycho at the end, there, didn't he?" Marty said.

"He's gonna regret it, too," Ben said. "You probably missed it with all the thunder and lightning and rain. But after he tomahawked the plate, the ump ejected him. Which means he's going to miss the first game of the playoffs."

"Bet the Yankees are thrilled about that," Marty said. "Their coach probably wanted to strangle him even before that."

"I actually felt sorry for Big Red when his mom came on the field and started yelling at their coach," Robbie said.

All three boys nodded somberly.

"Yeah," Marty said, "did you see the look on the kid's face? Like he wanted to crawl in a hole and die."

"I don't blame him," Ben said. "If my mom ever did that when I was playing, I'd never speak to her again."

"Yeah, right," Marty said. "Not until you needed her to drive you somewhere. Or wash your clothes. Or cook a meal. Or help with homework. Or give you money for iTunes. Or—"

"Okay, okay," Ben said, laughing. "I get the point."

"Maybe Big Red's mom was just having a bad day," Robbie said. "She probably didn't mean to embarrass him. Guess she thought she was protecting her kid."

"Here's a news flash for you," Marty said. "I'd be way more scared of her than of Big Red."

"I guess," Ben said. "But Big Red's the one throwing seventy-five-mile-per-hour fastballs at you during a game."

"Speaking of games," Robbie said, pointing to Ben, "you'll be playing in our league next year. Dad says you'll be one of the best players, too."

"I don't know," Ben said. "I got a lot of work to do before then."

"Look how quick you get the ball out of the glove now," Robbie said. "Go ahead, give us a little demonstration."

They stood and moved some ten feet apart. Robbie fired the ball at Ben, who caught it easily. He tucked his glove under the stump of his missing arm with a practiced motion and plucked the ball out smoothly before firing it back.

"Look at that!" Marty said. "You've totally got it down!"

Ben threw himself back on the grass, his face reddening. But Robbie and Marty could see he was pleased.

"Wouldn't it be great if we were all on the same team next year?" Marty said. "Robbie would be, like, the best pitcher in the league, now that he's not crazy anymore and worried about killing someone with a fastball."

"Thanks for being so sensitive," Robbie said, shaking his head.

"Ben would be the best hitter in the league," Marty

continued, "even with just one arm. And me, I'd be . . ." His voice trailed off.

"You just be you, Marty," Ben said. "That's good enough for us."

Marty smiled. "Well, remember that famous saying: 'Today you are You, that is truer than true. There is no one alive who is Youer than you.'"

"Okay, who said it?" Ben demanded. "Aristotle? Benjamin Franklin? Mark Twain?"

"Nope," Marty said, "that was my man Dr. Seuss."

"Close enough," Robbie said as they all laughed.

Then he jumped to his feet and threw another towering fly ball into the clear blue sky, a sky that looked near enough to touch.

If you enjoyed this book, look for

**SQUEEZE
PLAY**

a novel by

CAL RIPKEN, JR.
with Kevin Cowherd

Coming in Winter 2014